Forever Vows

The Lady in the Red Dress

On the Edge of Chance

Sealed with a Kiss

Kiss me at Midnight

The Heart Knows

Billionaire's Unexpected Landing

Billionaire's Accidental Girlfriend

Billionaire Fallen Angel

Billionaire's Secret Crush

Billionaire's Barefoot Bride

The Heart of Christmas

The Magic of Christmas

In a One Horse Open Sleigh

A Secret Royal Christmas

An Old-Fashioned Christmas

Second Chance Kisses

Second Chance Secrets

First Time Charm

Three Broken Rules

Second Chance Destiny

Unexpected Vows

Begin Again

Love Again

Falling Again

Just Stay

Just Chance

Just Believe

Just Us

Just Once

Just Happened

Just Maybe

Just Pretend

Just Because

Forever Vows

THE ASHTONS

FOREVER AND EVER

KATHRYN KALEIGH

FOREVER VOWS

PREVIEW THE PRINCESS AND THE PLAYBOY

Copyright © 2024 by Kathryn Kaleigh

All rights reserved.

Written by Kathryn Kaleigh.

Published by KST Publishing, Inc., 2024

Cover by Skyhouse24Media

www.kathrynkaleigh.com

Prologue

Little baby birds hidden away in a straw nest tucked in the fork of the old maple tree chirped shrilly for their mother.

"Can you see them?" Isabella asked, standing on her toes as though that would make her taller than her four feet two inches. She bounced on her white sneakers, swinging her blonde ponytail in the process.

"Almost," nine-year-old Daniel said, swinging dangerously to land on the next limb. "There."

"What do you see?" Isabella asked.

"There are five of them," Daniel said, looking down, grinning from ear to ear.

"Five. Wow."

"No. Wait. There are six of them. They're starving."

Isabella glanced over her shoulder.

"Come down," she said. "Before the mother sees you."

"I'm not afraid of a bird," he said. "Let's get some worms. Feed them."

Isabella put her hands on her hips. "You can't feed the birds," she said. "Just take the picture and come down."

"You're bossy for a girl," Daniel said, but he took his phone out of his pocket and snapped a picture."

"Come down," she said, bouncing again.

"Okay. Okay."

Daniel scooted nimbly from one limb to the other and he made his way down.

"You're going to fall," Isabella said.

Daniel landed nimbly on his feet.

"Didn't fall," he said, holding his arms over his head.

"You're an idiot," Isabella said, but she blew out a breath of relief.

"Your idiot," he said.

"Not mine."

"Wait. You said you'd be my girlfriend."

"That was before I found out you're an idiot."

She turned, facing the warmth of the sunshine on her face.

"Do you want to see the picture or not?"

"Yes!" She turned back, smiling. "Let me see."

"Girls," Daniel muttered under his breath, but he held up his phone.

Isabella took the phone and zoomed in on the little baby birds, their mouths wide open.

"Aw," she said. "They're really hungry."

"I told you."

The flutter of wings above signaled the return of the mother bird.

"She's back," Isabella said.

"Let's go," Daniel grabbed her arm to lead her away.

"But—"

"If she knows we're here, she won't feed them."

"Why, that's the silliest thing—"

But Daniel pulled her away where they crouched behind a purple blooming hydrangea bush.

"How do we know she's feeding them?" Isabella asked, worried now about the mother bird knowing Daniel had been in the tree. "Do you think she smells you?"

But Daniel, an always prepared boy scout, pulled his spyglass out of his back pocket and zoomed in on the birds.

"Look," he said. "She's feeding them."

"Aw," she said. "She's sharing her food. That is so amazingly wonderful."

Daniel watched Isabella carefully.

Satisfied, she lowered the spyglass and smiled at him.

"We can have six babies if you want."

"What?"

"Babies." Daniel sat back on his heels. "After we're married, of course."

"You don't want to marry me," Isabella said.

"I do. I'll marry you right now."

Isabella looked at him crossly and crossed her arms.

"There's no priest here."

"We don't need a priest. My sister said all you need to do is to say your vows."

"How does she know that?"

"She learned it in history class."

Isabella didn't really believe him. She had an older sister and three older brothers. If that was a thing, she would have heard about it.

But Daniel said it with the utmost conviction. And besides. He was looking at her with those smiling blue eyes that made her heart beat too fast.

"How?" Isabella asked, curiosity overcoming skepticism.

Daniel seemed to think for a minute.

"You don't know—"

"Put your hands in mine," he said holding out his hands, palms up.

She put her hands in his.

"Now what?"

"We say our vows." He took a breath. "I do."

Isabella had never been to a wedding, but she had seen weddings on television. So far, it seemed right to her. Right enough anyway.

"I do," she said. "So we're married now?"

"Not yet," he said. "There's one more thing we have to do to make it official."

"What's that?"

"I have to kiss you."

Isabella's eyes widened. Daniel Benton was going to kiss her.

"Are you sure?" She had imagined this moment about two million times. Since Kindergarten.

"If we don't, we won't be married."

Well, Isabella thought, she had come this far. Mimicking what she had seen on television, she closed her eyes, leaned forward at the waist, and puckered her lips.

Seconds passed. Two seconds. Three seconds.

Maybe she had misunderstood.

But then Daniel's lips lightly touched hers.

Opening her eyes, she grinned at him.

"We're married now."

"Yes," he said. "Forever and ever."

Chapter One

Isabella Ashton
Today

I UNROLLED the oversized vellum graph paper, spread it over the drafting table, and clipped it onto the top edge to keep it from sliding off.

Early morning sunlight streamed in through the third floor window of Ashton Manor, casting a bright glow of light across the desk.

My new studio. A quiet place just for me to work.

Maybe a little too quiet. I tapped my phone, turning on some popular music just loud enough to fill in some of that background quietness. Coming from a crowded corporate office environment, I had to get myself accustomed to the quiet.

Not quite happy with the light, I shoved the heavy hardwood desk, just a little, shifting it so that the paper was free from shadows.

The drafting table was new, but the desk behind me where I kept my rulers, pencils, paper, and other supplies was antique. It made a good desk for my computer, too.

The antique desk stayed put. It was so heavy, I couldn't move it if I had to.

It had been handed down through the years and according to my grandmother it had been built in the early 1800s and used by my great great great great grandfather who had built this house. She also told me that it had a secret compartment.

There were lots of stories about what was in that secret compartment, but no one knew for sure.

Everyone looked for the secret compartment. I looked for it, too. But no one could find it. I wasn't giving up on it. Someday I was going to figure it out.

On the lawn below, my sister-in-law's black retriever, basically a big oversized puppy, had been sniffing around for half an hour. Suddenly lifting his head, he raced toward the line of maple trees that indicated the end of the lawn and the beginning of the forest, toward something only he could see.

The dog came to an abrupt skidding stop at the edge of the lawn, about fifty yards across, at the maple trees, with their bright red leaves of fall, and laid his ears back.

Tori, the dog's owner, called him back. Biscuit. Tori and my brother James named their dog Biscuit. What happened to normal dog names like Charlie, Buddy, or Rover. Spot. Spot was a good name for a dog. Especially Biscuit since he had a white spot between his eyes.

If I had a dog, I'd name him Spot. Or maybe Bandit. Depending.

Personally, I was more of cat person. My best friend had a cat named Fluffy. A normal pet with a normal pet name.

Biscuit raced back toward the house on long gangly legs and disappeared beneath the terrace deck.

The back door closed below as they came inside.

With no more distractions outside, I sat on my drafting stool and sipped my hot latte.

Running a hand over the pristine sheet of paper, I considered where I wanted to start.

I had a rough sketch on a napkin. Something had come to me while I was having Sunday dinner with my family and instead of looking for sheet of real paper, I'd used the napkin at hand.

That's how it worked for me.

Ideas occurred to me when I was not supposed to be working—like Sundays with my family or showers. I got most of my ideas when I showered. Something about the hot water flowing over my head tended to loosen my thoughts.

The Ashton Manor was more than a house. It was an estate. I lived here with my parents, my four older siblings, and two sisters-in-law.

The house was so big we only saw each other in passing.

It would probably be different now, though, I mused, because starting today, I would be working from home.

Tori also worked from home, but she didn't have a studio. She liked working downstairs on the sectional sofa in front of the fireplace.

I'd worked on the kitchen table until today, but that had been when I'd worked from home after putting in hours at my full-time job.

I still couldn't believe I'd turned in my resignation and left my corporate job to go off on my own.

I was going on a leap of faith.

Doubling down on my idea of designing small cottage home offices for individuals. With so many people, professionals, working from home now, I saw the need for people having their own office space just steps away from their back doors.

A place they could call their own whether they wanted to work in the quiet or attend a Zoom meeting without the noises of family interrupting.

I'd only sold one of my plans, but I'd gotten a lot of interest.

Since it aligned with what I wanted to do, I took the leap.

One of my cousins out of Houston had put together a business plan for me. Ran some numbers.

And the result had been startling.

And yet I had not made the decision lightly.

I made pretty good money working at my corporate job. Decent, steady money.

But if my business made a go of it, I could make in one month what I would make in one year. My cousin had cautioned me that business success did not happen overnight.

I knew that, of course.

I also knew that at twenty-six, I had to make a move if I was going to.

So many people at my job were trapped. They had mortgages and car notes and children. They had too many obligations to leave the steady work force.

I'd personally spoken to a dozen people at work. They all told me the same thing.

If they had it to do over again, they would go out on their own before they became dependent on the money. I knew that ninety-nine percent of them would not do anything differently.

People tended not to take risks like that. They preferred the benefits and pension plan and steady income.

I had a safety net most people didn't have.

I had a place to live and no expenses.

My parents wouldn't let me fail. I might have to pivot, but I wouldn't fail. My grandfather owned several high rise buildings in Pittsburgh and establishments inside those buildings including five star restaurants. He provided the capital and other people ran the businesses.

He was exceptionally successful. His brother, my Uncle Noah, was also an entrepreneur. Uncle Noah had created the largest and most successful private airline company from the ground up. Skye Travels.

He had airplanes housed at various places around the country, including Pittsburgh.

That was my goal. I wanted to have my own architect firm with people working for me around the country. Or at least maybe in an office in the city.

I had entrepreneurship in my blood.

But first I had to start with my second blueprint.

I had to establish a brand before I could make sales. A lot of people thought it went the other way around. Most people wanted to find a client before they made blueprints.

I knew I had to have blueprints to attract clients, at least at first.

People had to see what they were buying, especially from someone without an established track record.

That would be me.

But if determination had anything to do with it, I would have lots of blueprints for people to choose from. I'd have a website that I'd already been working on. All I had to do now was to make the designs and put them up for sale.

I was betting on myself.

My phone chimed with a text message.

UNKNOWN NUMBER

> Hello. Isabella Ashton? I got your number from your neighbor. She said you might could held me design an office cottage for me.

My heart pounded rapidly in my chest.

This was happening much more quickly than I had planned.

Staring at the blank sheet of paper in front of me wasn't going to get the job done.

> Can we meet? To talk about what you have in mind.

Chapter Two

DANIEL Benton

I stepped off the elevator onto the second floor of the Skye Travels building at the edge of the Houston airport tarmac and turned toward Noah Worthington's office.

The thick carpet muffled the sound of my shoes. The offices were quiet. The only noise came from outside. The airplane engine on one side and the freeway traffic on the other side.

Noah Worthington was what I thought of as the big boss.

Didn't get much bigger in my mind.

Noah had started Skye Travels with one little Cessna airplane and built it into the largest private airline company in the country. He now had a fleet of airplanes including more Phenoms than any other one single man owned. Most of them were housed in Houston, but some were housed in various places around the country including Whiskey Springs and Mackinac Island. He had a tendency to go for places off the beaten path. Beautiful, magical places that didn't have easy access.

Of course, he also had airplanes in other cities, too, like Dallas and Birmingham.

Maggie, talking on her headset, as always, held up a hand in greeting as I passed. Maggie had been with Skye Travels for years. Some claimed she came with the place but Maggie always evaded giving a straight answer about that.

I walked down the hallway and stopped at Noah's door.

He turned around from where he stood looking out over the tarmac. He had the best view of the Houston Airport from here. He could see every one of his private jets as they came and went and if that wasn't enough, he could watch commercial jets landing and taking off on nearby runways. Most of them went airborne right over his office.

It was a befitting office for a man of Noah's stature and reputation.

I'd worked for Skye Travels for five years coming here straight after college graduation. The envy of most of my peers, many of whom took me off their friend list. It was my fault I landed one of the most coveted jobs for pilots.

Fortunately, I had friends who weren't pilots. I just didn't stay in touch nearly as much as I should.

"Come in," Noah said. "Have a seat."

In the five years that I had worked here at Skye Travels, I had never been summoned to his office. He'd interviewed me back when and that was that. I'd only seen him in passing since, at the office at least.

I'd been to his home for a couple of normal Sunday dinners and I'd been to holiday parties.

But I'd never once been summoned to his office.

If I had done something wrong, I couldn't imagine what it would be.

As I took a seat on the sofa in his little sitting area, a large commercial jet came in for a landing, the loud roar from its engines filling the air.

Noah didn't even seem to notice. He took two bottles of water from a little refrigerator and handed one to me. The water bottles had the red Skye Travels logo on the label.

"Thank you," I said, twisting the top off and drinking while I waited for him to fill me in on what he needed to talk to me about.

I shifted in my seat and adjusted my tie.

"You're not in trouble," Noah said, watching me.

Had I been that obvious?

"Good to know," I said.

"Actually I need a favor."

"A favor." I had not expected Noah Worthington to need a favor from me. I tended to fly beneath the radar.

Just doing my job and going home.

But I was a pilot and it was hard for a pilot to fly beneath the radar for very long.

"Sure thing," I said. "How can I help?"

I was thinking maybe he needed me to take an extra flight. Maybe an overnight flight. The married guys didn't like the extended overnight trips and Noah tried to accommodate them.

Being single, I didn't mind taking overnight trips, but he would know that. I took overnight trips all the time.

"You're originally from Pittsburgh, right?"

"Yes sir." I was still trying to figure out what kind of favor he might be looking for.

"Good," he said, stopping to watch one of his planes takeoff. He probably even knew who the pilot was. How many times had he watched me land and takeoff?

I waited in silence. He'd tell me in his own good time.

"I need someone to cover one of my Phenoms up there for a while."

"Pittsburgh?"

"Yes." He toyed with the label on his bottle of water.

"Okay. How long?"

"Two months."

"Oh. Two months."

I had an apartment. I had a little succulent that I'd had for ages. But I didn't have a girlfriend and I had a feeling he somehow knew that.

Noah knew everything there was to know about his people. Even those of us who stayed below the radar.

"You'll be provided an apartment and a car. All expenses covered."

I didn't doubt that.

"Why me?"

Noah smiled at me. An older man with silver in his hair, he still held himself tall and straight and could have passed for a much younger man.

In that smile, I could see the charm and persuasiveness that had no doubt helped him obtain the level of success he had achieved.

"Since you're from there," he said. "I thought you wouldn't

mind using the opportunity to go back. Spend some time with family."

Family. I still had a grandmother who lived in Pittsburgh, but my parents had retired to Florida. He would know that, of course.

A little tendril of fear wound its way through me.

"Has someone contacted you about my grandmother?" I asked, fearing the worst. Someone could have contacted me here about her. Not likely, but possible.

I should call her more often. She lived alone and as far as I knew there was no one to look in on her.

"No. No," Noah said, looking at me with concern now. "But it sounds like maybe you're thinking you might want to see how she's doing. If you decide to help me out on this."

"Of course," I said, scrubbing my chin. "I'd be happy to help you out."

"Good," Noah said. "That's good."

"I'll look in on my grandmother while I'm there."

Noah laughed.

"I'm sure she'll be happy to see you. Maggie will get you all the details."

With that, he stood up and walked back to the window."

"Is that all you needed, Mr. Worthington?"

"That's all," he said. "Thank you for helping out."

Still reeling from the strange conversation with the big boss, I went in search of Maggie.

My grandmother might be the only official family I had in Pittsburgh, but she wasn't the only person I had left behind.

Noah had really given me no choice.

I would be spending the next two months in my hometown.

Pittsburgh.

I was going home to Pittsburgh.

Not a big deal, I told myself. I would just take my plant with me. I could leave my car here at the airport in the Skye Travels parking lot.

I had lots of arrangements to make, but I was used to traveling on the fly.

I was a pilot. it's what I did.

Going back to Pittsburgh, though. That was not something I'd planned on doing.

First things first, I'd call Liam, my friend from college. Last I heard, he still lived in Pittsburgh.

The thought of spending two months there with no one to talk to but my grandmother didn't sound like something I wanted to do.

Chapter Three

ISABELLA

I recognized the name of my new client—my first private client—but I didn't recognize the address or the house.

The house was a large Georgian colonial-style house with what I thought of as a flat front. As an architect, I had a love hate relationship with the style. I loved it because it was iconic and symmetrical. All American.

Two stories. Two windows on either side. Kitchen in the back.

I hated it—too strong a word really—because as an architect, it was difficult to design something in that style that stood out from the crowd.

It was hard to create something different out of a classic design.

The house was freshly washed, letting the pale white brick shine through, belying its age.

Using the thick iron knocker, I knocked on the door and waited. A baby cried in the background and toddler screeched.

Maybe there was more than one Liam Johnson in Pittsburgh. It was more than a little bit possible. Likely.

The blonde woman who opened the front door had hair falling out of her ponytail. She looked harried and stressed, but she smiled at me.

I knew this woman. Somehow. I wasn't sure yet. But I knew her.

"Hi," she said and hearing her voice everything fit together and I recognized her.

"Hi." I smiled. "Melissa?"

"Yes?" With a toddler holding onto her right leg, she frowned at me with a mix of confusion and uncertainty.

"I'm Isabella Ashton," I said. "You contacted me or maybe your husband did."

"Isabella." Her face brightened. "The architect."

"Yes."

"Come in." I stepped inside after she opened the door. "I think... I think I know you." She watched me intently, trying to figure it out.

"You married Liam Johnson, right?" She nodded. "Your boyfriend was best friends with my... friend Daniel."

"Oh, of course," she said. "I have baby brain. I should have put that together."

"How would you?" I asked, giving her a break. From the looks of her house, she needed one.

"Come back to the kitchen," she said. "I have beanie weenies on the stove."

"People still eat those?" I mused.

"Three-year-olds do. I don't know about people."

I laughed.

"Have a seat," she said, picking up a teddy bear from one of the dining room chairs and setting it on top of the table.

As I sat down, she went back to the stove in the center of the island where she was stirring what did indeed smell like beanie weenies.

"I'm actually the one who contacted you."

"Oh. You work from home?" I tried to imagine Melissa getting any work done from anywhere, especially from here.

Besides the toddler attached to her leg, she had one in a playpen and if I was any judge at all, she had another one on the way.

She disentangled the toddler off her leg and set her in the dining room chair next to me.

The little girl looked at me as though she had never seen another human before.

"Hi," I said, getting no response.

"You design work cottages?" she asked, taking a pack of weenies from the refrigerator and proceeding to chop them into bite sized pieces.

"Yes," I said, gladly turning my attention back to Melissa. "I just —" I bit my tongue as I started to tell her that I had just started.

My mentor's words rang in my head. "Never let them know that you're new at what you do. As far as clients know, you are the expert."

She looked at me questioningly.

"I just wasn't sure what you all were looking for." I smiled.

"Liam doesn't know I contacted you," she said.

"Oh. I see." I didn't, but I would.

She slid the weenies off the cutting board and stirred them in with the beans.

"Liam is an attorney."

"Right. I remember he studied law."

"He has an office downtown, but he also does a lot of work from home." She glanced around. "I think he would do a lot more work at home if it was a little quieter." She lowered her voice as she neared the end of her sentence.

I glanced at the little girl. She was still watching me in silence.

"Hence the cottage office," I said. I hadn't decided for sure what I was going to call my little home office buildings, but right now cottage office seemed to fit.

"Yes," she said, enthusiastically. "Anything to keep my man at home, you understand?"

"Of course." Never let them know you're new and never let them know you didn't have a man.

She dipped up a spoonful of beanie weenies and put them on a blue plastic plate. Set it in front of the little girl.

"Do you want some beanie weenies?" she asked. "We have plenty."

"No," I said quickly, "but thank you."

Melissa put a scoop of beanie weenies on another saucer and sat down at the table with it.

"Eat," she told the little girl, then proceeded to do so herself.

"Sorry to eat in front of you," she said. "But I have a Zoom call in thirty minutes.

"No need to apologize," I said, fascinated at not only seeing an adult eating beanie weenies, but also that the little girl did as she was told.

Being the youngest of five siblings, I didn't know a whole lot about children, but Melissa made chaos look easy.

"How much space are you thinking?" I asked, glancing out the back window at what, from here, looked like a massive back yard. Plenty of room to put a cottage office.

"I don't know," Melissa said with a little shrug.

I didn't remember her being so laid back in college. Maybe having two and a half children did that to a person.

"Can you put together some designs? You know. A starting place? And we can go over them from there?"

"Of course. I didn't bring anything today. I was just hoping to get a general idea of size and scope."

Melissa finished off her beanie weenies. Took the plate to the sink, rinsed it, and put it in the dishwasher.

"Just think attorney," she said.

"Will he have clients come here?"

"Maybe," she said. "Probably. A lot of Zoom calls, but clients might come here."

I was wondering if maybe she shouldn't ask him, but she obviously wanted it to be a surprise. I would use what information I had to start with.

"I can pay you by the hour," she said. "What's your rate?"

Fortunately, I was prepared to answer that question. I told her my rate.

"Okay," she said without a blink. I had been afraid that it was a little high. I was asking more per hour than I had made at my corporate job. All at the advice of my cousin in Houston.

"Just text me an invoice. I'll pay you for today. I really have to get ready for my call. When can you come back?"

I opened up my calendar app. My time was wide open, but I didn't tell her that. I calculated how much time I would need to put together the first outline of a sketch.

"I have time Friday afternoon," I said.

"Perfect. Text me if you have any questions between now and then."

"Do you mind if I use the back door so I can get a feel for the space?"

"Not at all," she said. "That's a great idea. There's a stone walkway that leads around to the front."

She somehow managed to herd me to the door without it feeling like I was being dismissed, although I was.

"I'll see you on Friday," she said.

Feeling like I had just been through a whirlwind, I stood outside the back door of the colonial style house, the door closed behind me and tried to regroup.

So my client was the Liam Johnson I had known from college... or rather his wife.

I hadn't considered that I would be designing a surprise cottage office for someone. That added a whole different level to things.

Even more levels came from knowing the clients. Or more specifically from knowing them when they were college students.

I wouldn't let that affect anything though.

I considered the space they had for the building. Imagined the little cottage tucked among the maple trees.

A lot of people would want to cut trees to make a clean area to build. I didn't believe in that. I would work around the trees. Let them stand.

Maybe even find a way to bring the outdoors inside.

The beauty of it was if the Johnsons didn't like the design, I could sell it to someone else. And on top of that, I would get paid for putting together the design.

That was unexpected and nice.

I took a few photographs. Some mental measurements. There was plenty of room to work with.

When I came back Friday, I would bring a tape measure and do some actual measurements.

Using the stone walkway to make my way around front, I considered that they already had a built-in entrance for clients. Clients wouldn't even have to go inside the main house. I imagined a little sign out front with Liam's name, instructed them to follow an understated arrow.

Considering the chaos created by children in there, that was most definitely a good thing.

This was good.

A very good challenge.

Chapter Four

DANIEL

The thing about men was that they could be best friends and not talk to each other for thirty years. Just pick right back up where they left off like they'd seen each other yesterday.

It hadn't been that long since I'd seen Liam, but the concept still applied. It applied even though he now had two children and one on the way.

"You know you can always stay with us," Liam said as I climbed inside his brand new BMW sedan. Solid white with dark leather seats.

"Thanks," I said. "But no thanks. Nice car." It had that new car smell and even though he had those two children, no one would ever know it. No car seat in the back. I would bet money that the little ones didn't ride in the BMW. Either that or he had a really good detailing service.

"Thanks. You don't like children, do you?"

"I can honestly say I know very little about the little people."

Liam laughed.

"You would learn," he said. "You would learn quickly, but that's okay. I'll break you in slowly."

I looked at him sideways. I had not considered that my best friend from college would have two children and one on the way. I had also not considered that he would feel compelled to indoctrinate me into his world of fatherhood.

He pulled out onto the freeway, driving me toward my apartment which just so happened to be only a few miles from Liam's house.

Convenient, but Liam would have picked me up anyway and driven me across town if need be. That's how guys were.

"Do you have a flight Friday?"

"I don't have my schedule yet." Maybe that was for the best.

"So if you don't have a flight, come by Friday afternoon. We'll grill some steaks."

"I'll let you know," I said. "Thanks." I reminded myself that I was the one who had contacted Liam. I was the one who didn't want to spend two months by myself.

"How's your grandmother?"

"I'm going by tomorrow to check on her."

"Yeah. I can't believe your parents just up and moved to Florida. Left her here."

"From what I hear, she didn't want to go. Too hot."

Liam laughed.

"Isn't that why old people move to Florida?"

"Hell if I know."

"I can't wait for you to meet my kids," Liam said. "I'd spend more time at home, but you know, it's a catch-22. Too much noise to get work done."

"I'm sure you'll figure something out."

"Yeah, with number three on the way, I'm not sure that's going to happen."

"How's Melissa in all this?"

"I swear the woman has no stress."

"That's not how I remember her."

"I know. Right? She's like a natural born mother."

"I think my apartment is right up there," I said, keeping an eye on my GPS.

"Call me if you need anything at all."

"Don't worry," I said. "You're my closest known neighbor."

He pulled up to the door. "I'm glad you're here. We'll have a beer and catch up."

"I can't wait," I said. "Thanks for the ride."

I piled out of the car, grabbed my luggage from the trunk, and headed for the apartment office. Everything was supposed to be taken care of. I even had a key already, but apparently there was something I had to sign.

An adventure. It was going to be an adventure.

And besides just work, I had some things I needed to take care of while I was here.

One of them was visiting my grandmother.

The other one was far more complicated.

And I wasn't ready for it yet.

Chapter Five

ISABELLA

Bent over my drafting table, I captured the outline of my idea.

The light was just right. Coming in through the window, splashing across my drafting paper.

My pencil moved quickly over the paper, trying to keep up with my brain.

I measured. Considered. Measured some more.

Sitting back, I put my pencil in my mouth and turned my paper around.

I had found a way to incorporate the maple trees, making a little courtyard in the middle of the office cottage. It would be a good place for a child to play in the mid-day sunshine. Or a great place for a cat. Add some flowers to attract butterflies. Add a normal cat named Fluffy and it was perfect.

For Liam Johnson, I imagined a toddler laughing and chasing after a puppy while he worked at his desk overlooking the courtyard.

There would only be one door leading out to the courtyard, so even if Liam got engrossed in his work, he didn't have to worry about his child running off out of sight.

I didn't know much about children, but I imagined it was a really good design. I'd incorporated both the maple trees and their children's safety and I was only getting started.

Someone drove up and parked at the back door. One of my brothers.

I glanced at the big clock on the wall behind me.

Time had gotten away from me.

I stood up and stretched. Realized I had been having fun. It was fun to design what I wanted to design. To focus on the needs of my client and come up with something unique just for them. Their needs. Their space.

It was time to stop for dinner. I might come back in a little while and do some more work on the design, but right now it was time for dinner and my stomach was growling.

I put my rulers and pencil away in the antique desk and pulled a dried leaf off the yellow daffodil in a vase in the middle of the desk.

As I headed downstairs thinking about what the little office cottage might look like on the inside and thinking about how I might decorate it, it occurred to me that my sister Charlotte would be perfect for that part of the job.

Charlotte and I could work together. I wondered why it hadn't occurred to me before to bring Charlotte into my new company. I was so focused on making my own move to working for myself that I hadn't thought about Charlotte.

Charlotte was an artist at heart, but she had gone the university professor route in order to have a steady income. Benefits. All that.

Her artistic flair overflowed into interior decorating, but she didn't do much with it. It was more of a hobby. A hobby that could easily be more.

I never quite understood how my quintessential entrepreneur grandfather's spirit had gotten twisted into such traditional work ethics as it passed to his son who then passed those traditional work ethics to his five children.

Maybe I just thought he had. Maybe I had entrepreneurial blood running through my veins, too that I was just now learning about.

I was so caught up in my thoughts that I nearly ran headlong into my oldest brother at the foot of the stairs.

"Hey," James said.

"Hey. Make some noise next time."

"Didn't you hear me drive up?"

I rolled my eyes at him.

"Not the same thing."

"Anyway," he said. "I was coming up to look for you."

"What for?" I asked, continuing toward the kitchen to grab a bottle of cold water from the refrigerator. I took one. Handed another to my brother.

"I was looking at my schedule today and guess who's on there." He sat on one of the bar stools, his long legs stretched out in front of him.

"I don't know."

My head was still in my design and on the possibility of bringing

Charlotte onboard, part time, of course. She was tenure track and nobody could persuade her away from that.

"Guess," he said.

"I don't know," I said again, climbing onto the bar stool next to him. Sometimes James would tell me about famous or important people that he piloted around in his airplanes. Pilots, it seemed, had no confidentiality clause. Not with sisters at any rate.

"Daniel."

I froze, the water bottle halfway to my lips.

"Daniel?" There were a lot of Daniels. I tried to remember if James had told me about any famous Daniels.

"Daniel Radcliffe?"

James shot me a look.

There was only one Daniel that I knew. Certainly only one that I was well acquainted with.

"Daniel Benton," he said.

"Our friend?"

"Do you know another Daniel Benton?" James went to the refrigerator, pulled out a loaf of cheese and dragged the cheese cutter out of the drawer.

This was not the time for James to be difficult.

"He chartered a private flight?"

James frowned at me over his shoulder.

"As a pilot," he said.

I didn't say anything. I knew that Daniel was a pilot. James knew I knew. Daniel had spent more time at our house than his own until he had moved away for college.

"Why?" I asked, ignoring the plate of sliced cheese that James set on the island in front of us.

It was an unnecessary question, but it was the only word I seemed to be able to vocalize at the moment. My heart was racing a hundred miles an hour.

James shrugged and popped a bite of cheese in his mouth.

"Thought maybe you would know."

Of course he thought I would know. Daniel and I had been close friends. Or at least I thought we had been.

I hadn't heard from him since he left for college.

That had been eight years.

Eight years since I had seen Daniel Benton.

By my best estimate, it had been about eight minutes since he had crossed my mind.

Chapter Six

DANIEL

Turns out I did not have a flight on Friday. I didn't, in fact, have any flights all week.

Apparently there was a transition period rife with paperwork before I could start flying.

That was unexpected. I thought Skye Travels was Skye Travels. It had something to do with Pennsylvania, but I didn't really ask.

Instead, I spent my two days off with my grandmother.

First of all, her house was a wreck. From the minute I pulled into the driveway, I knew the walls needed painting on the outside.

I could take care of that for her.

I wasn't, however, prepared for what I found on the inside of the house.

Grandma was happy to see me and she seemed both in good

health and content, but things around her house were broken. Broken and in serious need of upkeep. That happened, though, when a woman lived alone, especially an older woman whose husband had always taken care of such things.

It wasn't that she didn't know who I was, but since I was family, she seemed to think that I was here to fix things for her.

Two light bulbs that required a ladder to replace were burned out. Fortunately Grandma didn't try to climb a ladder to change them herself.

One of her stove burners wasn't working and there was something wrong with her air conditioning. She was running a window unit. I didn't know anything about air conditioning but I could figure it out or I could find someone who did know how to fix it.

I took notes of everything that needed to be done and another list of everything I needed to buy at the hardware store.

Paint. Air conditioning filters. A new interior door knob.

As I was leaving, I realized she needed new external door locks, too.

By the time I finished I had a page and a half of supplies I needed to buy before I could even get started on her repairs.

I was thinking I was going to need more than two months to fix everything that she needed to have fixed, especially if I did all the painting myself.

Fortunately, she wasn't lonely. She had a neighbor, also an elderly lady, who visited her every day. The two of them ran whatever errands they needed to do together. So at least there was that.

Friday morning, before I headed over to Liam's house, I dropped off a load of the first of many supplies.

Grandma insisted on making sandwiches for us.

After lunch, I went ahead and changed her front door locks. Programed in a code for her and taught her how to use it.

Feeling accomplished about crossing something off my list, I headed over to Liam's house.

He lived in an established neighborhood with evidence of lots of old money. He was doing well for himself as an attorney.

I pulled into the circle drive of Liam's Georgian colonial-style house and parked, then double-checked the address.

His BMW had to be hidden in the garage, so I had no clues that I was actually in the right place. There was another car, a small silver Mercedes sitting in the circle drive. Probably a friend of Melissa's.

Somehow I'd never pictured Liam living in a house like this and to be quite honest, it made me feel rather unsuccessful to be living in a one bedroom apartment.

There was a reason for those differences, I reminded myself.

First of all, Liam was an attorney and I was a pilot. As a pilot, I spent most of my time in the air or in hotels in other cities.

I didn't know what I would do with a house like this if I had it.

It would be nice though. I had the skills needed to take care of a house.

Maybe one day.

Second of all, Liam had a wife and children. A man, whether he was an attorney or a pilot, needed a nice house like this for a family.

If I had a wife and children, I would not let them live in an apartment. I would have a nice house for them in a nice area.

Maybe one day.

Grabbing the six pack of beer I had brought to go with the steak Liam would be grilling, I got out of the car.

The wind, knocking red leaves from the maple trees, had a chill to it, an early precursor of the winter to come.

Maybe he would change his mind about grilling outside. Besides being chilly, it was cloudy and dreary.

In the years I had spent living in Houston, I had grown accustomed to bright sunny days for grilling.

Cloudy days were few and far between.

Of course, having grown up here, I knew that cloudy days were the norm in Pittsburgh.

It would take some readjusting to get used to it again. I wasn't sure I wanted to live in a cloudy, dreary place again.

But it was just two months.

Two months and I would be back in Houston in time for the annual Christmas fireworks.

"Liam," Melissa said, opening the door as I approached. "How are you? It's been a long time."

"It has, hasn't it?" I gave her a quick hug.

Melissa had changed since I'd seen her in college.

Part of it, I decided, was because she was several months pregnant. The other, I decided, was because she looked tired.

Did Liam know that she needed help? A nanny maybe.

Surely they had a housekeeper, though by the looks of things, if they did, it was the housekeeper's day off.

Toys were strewn everywhere.

"Liam isn't home yet," she said. "Tied up at work. Again." She made a face.

"I can come back," I said. there was a squealing toddler somewhere in the house. I wasn't ready for that.

"Nonsense," she said. "There's someone here you'll want to see."

"Sure," I said, not wanting to be rude to my best friend's wife, especially not when I hadn't seen her in years.

"Let me take that," she said, taking the six pack of beer out of my hands. "I'll put these in the freezer."

"Right." I had forgotten that Liam also liked his beer lightly frozen.

One of many thing he and I had in common.

"Come on back to the kitchen," she said with a mischievous gleam in her eyes.

Wary, I followed her.

A young lady with a high ponytail sat at her kitchen table, papers spread out in front of her.

"If you have a guest," I said. "I can come back."

She ignored me this time, stashing two bottles of beer in the freezer and putting the rest in the refrigerator.

"Have a seat anywhere," Melissa said.

Heading toward a bar stool, one of few places that didn't have toys on it, I stopped to speak to the girl sitting at the table.

Looking up at me, her eyes wide, her gaze locked onto mine.

"Bella?" I asked.

"Daniel?"

I all but forgot that Melissa was even in the room.

Straightening, she looked at me as though she was seeing a ghost.

Not exactly the warm reunion I had envisioned in my head.

Chapter Seven

ISABELLA

With one knee on a wooden chair, I leaned over my blueprints spread out on Melissa's round breakfast table.

The house smelled like warm milk and butterscotch. I got the warm milk part, but the butterscotch was an unknown.

I soon learned that Melissa's three-year-old daughter's name was Grace. Grace carted around a kitten, she called Pooh. Apparently Grace's grandmother had brought her the kitten yesterday and the kitten's feet had barely touched the ground since.

I'd been on the right track when I had envisioned a cat in Liam's office cottage. A cat and a child.

Since I got there an hour ago, Grace had been sitting quietly on the sofa watching something on television. Cartoons, I think, of some sort. Not the cartoons of my childhood.

When someone drove up out front, Grace got up and ran to the kitchen, the kitten still clutched in her arms. Her loud squealing woke up the baby sleeping in a bassinet near the window.

So much for silence.

So now we had a squealing toddler and a crying baby in addition to a ringing doorbell.

I wondered if I should do something. I could turn on the mobile over the baby's bassinet, but I was hesitant to touch anything related to the baby.

Surely I wasn't supposed to pick her up.

That was the thing about having four old brothers and sisters. They had babysat me, but I'd had no one to babysit.

I would just wait. Melissa would be back shortly.

As Melissa went to answer the door, Grace sat down at the table and stared at me, much as she had done the first time I visited.

Melissa had a guest, but that didn't concern me.

Not knowing what to say to Grace, I just shrugged and went back to adding the closet that Melissa wanted.

I was here with Melissa with clear instructions to put away the blueprints when Liam got home.

Unfortunately he was running late and the later he ran, the more time Melissa had to scrutinize my blueprints and suggest changes.

She seemed to like the design overall, but she was more hands on than I had hoped. So I added in the closet. Leaned back to study it. The closet was actually a good idea.

"Have a seat anywhere," Melissa said, going straight to the bassinette to pick up and soothe the crying baby.

Straightening, I looked up to see who was joining me.

I knew the second I saw him.

That face. Those eyes. That smile.

That voice.

"Bella?"

My heart jumped out of my skin and landed somewhere in my throat.

"Daniel."

I knew he was back. My brother had warned me that he was back.

Seeing Daniel today had not been on my list of the day's possibilities.

I'd thought I might see him at some point, but I honestly couldn't imagine how that situation would come about.

I didn't go to the airport. I certainly didn't fly private even if had somewhere to go.

He had no reason to visit me at my house. It would actually be a little bit strange if he did show up out of the blue, especially since I hadn't heard from him in years.

He probably didn't even still have my phone number.

He started to step forward, then noticed Grace sitting there, and stopped.

"Hi," he said, his eyes back on mine.

"Hi."

Moving as though it was the most normal thing in the world, he swept up the teddy bear that had ended up back in one of the chairs and sat down.

"What are you doing?" he asked, casually holding that teddy bear in his lap.

"What?" Something about Daniel holding that bear had me off balance.

He glanced down at the blueprints. "Blueprints."

"Oh I..." I glanced over at Melissa.

Liam and Daniel were friends. If Liam wasn't supposed to know about the office cottage, then I couldn't imagine that Daniel was supposed to know either.

"Nothing," I said, quickly rolling up the blueprints. "I was just going over something with Melissa."

"Building house for Daddy."

I stopped, holding the rolled up blueprint in both hands.

I looked over at Melissa, but she was soothing the baby and hadn't heard her daughter's words.

"No," I said, shaking my head and forcing a little smile. "Not a house."

Daniel was watching me with an amused expression.

"It's a surprise," I said, glancing at Daniel. "I can't tell you."

"Okay."

"We can't tell your daddy," I told Grace.

Grace just shrugged and squeezed her kitten.

"Daddy!" Grace jumped up at the sound of the garage door opening.

"Liam is home," Melissa said over her shoulder. When I saw the blanket over her shoulder, I realized that she was nursing the baby.

"I should go." I grabbed my leather tube and started shoving the blueprints inside.

"No," Melissa said. "Liam saw your car. It would look suspicious for you to leave now."

"He doesn't know my car," I said, but she was right. It would look suspicious and she would have to explain it away.

"Sit," she said. "Stay. It'll be like old times."

I looked over at Daniel as I dropped into the chair.

Liam came in through the garage door and grabbed Grace up, kitten and all.

"What have you got there?" he asked her.

"Pooh." Grace giggled.

It was the first time I'd heard the little girl laugh.

After Liam kissed his wife, Melissa took the kitten from their daughter's grasp and set it in front of a bowl of food.

The little kitten put one paw in the bowl and started eating.

"Looks who's here," Melissa said. "Daniel and Bella."

"Bella," Liam said, giving me a quick side hug. "It's good to see you."

He looked questioningly over at Daniel.

Daniel just looked at him.

I couldn't tell either one of them why I was here.

It was most awkward.

Chapter Eight

DANIEL

It was a little like stepping into an alternate universe. I'd known that Daniel and Melissa had gotten married. I'd been to the wedding. I also knew they had children.

Even knowing that Liam was an attorney didn't make it any less strange seeing him in his charcoal gray business suit with light gray tie and shiny black shoes. He looked good. Successful.

His wife looked tired, but now that Liam was home, she looked a little less tired. Looked brighter. That told me a lot.

Being here. Seeing them in their life with children would take a little getting used to.

Bella being here just added to that surreal feeling.

Bella and I had never dated.

It wasn't because I didn't want to date her. We just hadn't.

I had met Liam my second year of college and we had been best friends since. Liam and Melissa had already been dating by then.

Bella had joined up at college the next year, but she had only stayed for one semester before transferring.

I never knew what happened.

I could have found out. I knew where she lived, but I'd been busy. Being an aviation student had taken all my energy. And any energy I had left I had used hanging out with Liam and sometimes Melissa.

I had quite simply let Bella walk right out of my life. To be quite honest, when Bella had transferred, I'd been dating a girl whose name I couldn't even remember.

Bella always seemed so out of my league. She was pretty. She was smart. And she was classy.

While Liam and I were out drinking beer, she was going to soirees and galas.

As an Ashton, she ran in different circles than I did.

We'd been friends when we were children, but time had taken us in different directions.

One of the things I had planned on doing while I was here was seeing Bella.

I just hadn't figured out how I was going to go about it.

I was still calculating an excuse to see her.

But here she was. Sitting in Liam's kitchen.

Working on something with Liam's wife.

Something Liam wasn't supposed to know about.

She'd tried to dart out when Liam came home, but Melissa hadn't let her.

Melissa and Liam were a couple. I'd simply accepted it and never given her much thought one way or the other. But right at this particular moment, she was one of my favorite people.

I'd come here to hang out with Liam—to catch up, but now that Bella was here with us, the evening took on a whole different hue.

"I brought steaks," Liam said, handing a paper bag to Melissa.

Then he turned Grace upside, making her squeal.

"Have you met this little person?" he asked me.

"Sort of," I said, not sure of the proper protocol for meeting a child.

Liam put Grace on her feet. She scampered off to do whatever three-year-old children did.

"I need to change clothes, then we'll heat up the grill," Liam said.

"No problem."

After he headed upstairs to change, Melissa took two bottles of beer out of the freezer. Handed one to me and one to Bella. Added another one in.

With a quick glance over her shoulder, Melissa kept her voice low.

"Okay," she said. "Liam can't know the real reason Bella is here."

"What's the real reason?" I asked.

"I'll tell you later," she said. "But now, just do me a favor and pretend... something."

"Pretend what?" Bella asked.

"Pretend to be together," she said. "You dated, right?"

We both said no at the same time.

"Well, you should have."

"I need to at least take these out to the car," Bella said.

"Okay," Melissa said, distracted by the whimpering of her baby.

Bella strapped the leather tube over her shoulder and headed out the front door.

"You can't tell me what's going on?" I asked Melissa. Secrets were never my strong point.

"Not now," she said impatiently. "Two people might can keep a secret, but not three."

"Alright," I said, stretching out my legs and taking a sip of my beer.

"Thank you."

"Do you think Bella's coming back?" I asked, noticing her beer sitting untouched on the table.

"Maybe you should go see."

I didn't move.

"You do know it's been about eight years since we've seen each other, right?"

Melissa blinked innocently. "Has it been that long?"

I rolled my eyes at her.

"When is your baby due?"

"March," she said, without a blink.

The front door opened, signaling that Bella was coming back in. At about the same time, Liam came back down the stairs.

"Let's get this party started," he said, rubbing his hand together.

I wasn't excited about going outside to grill steaks to begin with, but now that Bella was here, I was even less excited to leave her. Unfortunately, I didn't see that I had a choice.

I followed Liam outside into the cold to watch him heat up his grill, but my thoughts were on Bella.

Chapter Nine

ISABELLA

While I was outside, I sent a quick text to my mother telling her it looked like I wouldn't be home for dinner.

Our family tried to have dinner together when at all possible. My mother insisted it was one of the things that held our family together.

The tradition had started with my grandparents. They had made some mistakes when they were young that had alienated them from their families. They were determined not to let us make the same mistakes.

When I got back inside the kitchen, Daniel was already out back with Liam.

Melissa stood at the island, tearing up lettuce for a salad.

"Thanks for staying," she said.

"Sure. I don't mean to intrude."

"You aren't intruding," she said. "We're happy to have you. Besides, it's nice to talk to someone over the age of three."

"You've got Liam," I pointed out, sitting down and picking up my beer. I didn't normally drink beer, but the frosty part at the top was interesting.

"Yeah. Well. Someone over the age of three who speaks about things unrelated to all things legal."

"I've forgotten," I said. "What did you major in?"

"Psychology."

"My oldest brother James is married to a psychology professor."

"I didn't know that," she said, moving on to cutting carrots on a cutting board.

"She teaches mostly online now."

"I'd like to go back to get my Ph.D. someday."

"I think you should."

"Not likely," she said with a glance around to indicate her children.

"Tori says most Ph.D. students are older and a lot of them have families," I said. "So never say never."

Melissa rinsed a colander full of small tomatoes, then began chopping them up with enviable skill.

"I'll keep that in mind," she said.

"You said you had a Zoom call the other day, so you're doing something, right?"

"Family." Melissa waved it off. "Our father has some dementia, so my mother talks to me and my sister as we try to figure out how to deal with it."

"I'm so sorry to hear that, Melissa," I said. I couldn't imagine the heartbreak that must come along with that.

She just shrugged.

"It's one of those things that comes with adulting, right?"

I took another sip of the frosty beer.

Melissa was a year older than me at most. Her version of adulting was so much different from mine. She was married with two children and one on the way. She had the big house. Was successful enough that she was building a separate home office for her husband—as a surprise, so they obviously didn't have to discuss such a large expenditure. And she was dealing with older parent issues.

My current adulting was living at home with my parents, leaving my corporate world job and getting my independent career off the ground.

I wasn't even dating anyone.

I glanced out the window at Daniel standing next to the grill with Liam.

He looked good. A little bit taller than when I had last seen him. Maybe a little more muscular. Nothing too obvious, but a hint of muscles rippled beneath his white cotton button down shirt.

He'd moved from being a cute boy into what I described as a handsome man. His jawline was more angular and he held himself with the confidence of a man as opposed to the uncertainty of a college freshman.

I had liked him since I was nine years old. Our fathers had worked together, so they'd gotten together some, rather like Daniel and Liam were doing today except Daniel's father brought his family.

Then we had grown up and stopped being required to go where our parents went. I think Daniel's parents lived in Florida now.

"Would you take these potatoes out to Liam?" Melissa asked, handing me a tray of foil wrapped potatoes.

"Sure." I'd been busted watching the guys anyway.

Melissa just smiled as I headed out the back door.

Chapter Ten

DANIEL

The cold wind didn't seem to bother Liam. He was obviously used to it.

In the years I had spent as a Houstonian, I had become more accustomed to warm weather and less acclimated to the cold.

Their backyard was big. Half the size of a football field which was surprisingly big considering the neighborhood. It was, however, an old neighborhood designed back when lots were bigger. This neighborhood had probably been out in the country just a few decades ago at most.

The yard was dotted with old maple trees, their leaves a beautiful bright red—in their most beautiful state before falling to the ground in winter's icy grip.

I was impressed that they hadn't cut the old trees down. A lot of people felt compelled to have a clean treeless yard. I saw no point in cutting down trees for no reason.

Without trees there was no place for the birds to build nests.

And no place for eager little boys to climb in order to impress pretty little girls.

The grown up version of that pretty little girl I'd just been thinking about walked out the back door carrying a tray loaded with baked potatoes wrapped in foil.

"You've got enough food here for ten people," I told Liam as I took the tray out of Bella's hands.

"Melissa has a tendency to overdo things. We'll have leftovers for a week."

"Hard to complain about that," I said.

Then I remembered that Bella and I were supposed to be pretending to date.

"Thank you," I said, putting an arm around Bella, pulling her close, happily getting the hug I hadn't gotten when I walked into the kitchen. A side hug was better than no hug.

She'd heard Melissa ask us to pretend to be together. She hadn't agreed or disagreed, but she didn't resist. In fact, she put her arm around me, too.

Liam seemed to think nothing of us standing there wrapped in each other's arms.

I, on the other hand, was keenly aware. All my nerve endings tingled.

Bella looked up at me with those green eyes. Her eyes reminded me of the Morning Glory Pool at Yellowstone National Park. Beautiful. Deep. And deadly to fall into.

I had a feeling that if I fell into Bella's eyes, I would never find my way out.

Not that I would want to find my way out.

When she smiled at me, my heart did a summersault and landed somewhere in my throat.

"Would you watch the grill for a minute?" Liam asked. "I need to step inside. Be right back."

"Sure."

After Liam was inside, I released my hold on Bella and leaned back against the porch railing.

"Melissa wants us to pretend to be together," I said. "Do you know what that's about?"

"Not really," she said, looking across the maple tree studded lawn.

"Huh. There must be a reason."

Bella blew out a breath.

"She has a surprise for Liam. I can't tell you."

"It has something to do with blueprints," I said.

She smiled that smile that lit up her whole face and reminded me of the sirens who lured sailors onto the rocks where they met their death.

"Has anyone ever told you that you have deadly eyes?"

Chapter Eleven

ISABELLA

I wasn't much of an outdoor person, all things considered.

I rather liked watching falling snow through a window next to the warmth of fireplace.

At the moment though, being outside in the cold, I wasn't complaining.

I couldn't even say that I noticed the cold at the moment.

What I noticed instead was the heat coming off of Daniel.

When he'd held me close, I felt warm. And safe.

It was so incredibly odd because I had never hugged Daniel.

I'd kissed him once, when I was nine years old, but I had never been in his arms.

It was all very... unexpected.

I looked into his blue eyes, eyes that reminded me of a clear summer sky, and tumbled right over.

The cute little boy I'd had a serious crush on as a child was now a good looking handsome man.

By the time I was old enough to understand what having a boyfriend meant, Daniel was already dating. His good looks and easy-going charm attracted girls. Cheerleaders. Homecoming queen. I never knew him to have a particularly serious relationship, but he always had dates.

And the thing about it was, he never asked me out.

"Has anyone ever told you that you have deadly eyes?"

"What?" I asked, thinking I had surely misunderstood him.

"Deadly eyes."

"No. I can't say that anyone has ever told me that," I said. "And I am more than a little bit confused."

"Are you aware of the story of the sirens who lured the sailors onto the rocks where they met their demise?"

I leaned back against the railing next to him.

"I never really understood that," I said.

"What's not to understand?"

"Odysseus was the only man who ever heard them and lived to tell about it, right?" I took a sip of my beer. Winced. Beer was not my drink of choice.

"So the legend goes."

I nodded. Looked out across the lawn and imagined how it would look after they built the little office cottage I had designed for Liam.

"You're not a beer drinker, are you?" Daniel asked.

"No." I glanced down at the bottle. I'd only sipped the icy part. "I've never had a frozen beer."

"Makes them tolerable," he said.

My gaze locked onto his. And for a moment, the rest of the world faded away.

If anyone was a siren, he was.

"I don't sing," I said.

He laughed. "You don't have to sing, sweetie."

Liam came back out with a plate of steaks ready to put on the grill.

"These are going to be good," he said, looking from one of us to the other. "Everything okay?"

"Yes," Daniel said.

I nodded, but I was still processing Daniel Benton calling me sweetie.

Even the Daniel Benton I had created in my mind out of a blend of memories and imagination didn't call me sweetie.

I couldn't, though in all fairness, say that my fantasies involved very much conversation.

My mind was racing in about fifty different directions.

I did not have a blueprint for this particular situation.

I was just here to design an office cottage for Liam. Secretly.

And now I was standing in their backyard while Liam was grilling steaks.

Standing next to Daniel.

I was beginning to worry that Daniel was different from the person I had imagined.

I had not seen Daniel for about nine years or so and I had never been on a date with Daniel.

There was no reason for him to call me sweetie. I struggled with it, but I couldn't come up with one.

So by deduction, if he called me sweetie, he must call all girls sweetie. There were guys—lots of guys—like that.

He might not be singing, but I had a very sneaky feeling that he might actually be the siren calling me over toward the deadly rocks.

Chapter Twelve

DANIEL

Bella didn't say much during dinner and neither did I.

Fortunately, Melissa and Liam didn't seem to notice. The conversation flowed with Bella and I not having to say all that much.

It helped that they were distracted by their baby who was colicky.

"We're so sorry about the baby," Melissa, looking harried again, said as we finished up what was a really good grilled steak dinner.

"You don't need to apologize," I said. "Why don't the two of you go on up? Do what you need to do while I stay and clean up?"

"Don't be ridiculous," Liam said. "You're a guest. We can't ask you to clean the kitchen."

"You didn't ask," I said. "I'm here and you need help."

I still maintained that they needed a nanny and/or a housekeeper and I saw no indication that they had either one of those. They needed help more than they needed whatever Bella was designing for them.

It wasn't, however, my place to say so.

But I could help out while I was here.

"I'll stay and help, too," Bella said.

Melissa and Liam exchanged a glance. Liam shook his head, but Melissa gave a little shrug.

"Only if you'll stay for a while and make yourselves at home. Have a date night."

I glanced at Bella. She had a deer in the headlights look in her eyes.

"Go," I said. "Don't worry about us."

Taking their colicky baby and their three-year-old who had been quietly playing in the floor with her kitten, they left us and went upstairs.

"You don't have to stay," I told Bella.

"It would look rather bad if I didn't, wouldn't it?"

"Not to me," I said. "You just sort of inadvertently got caught up in this."

"It was my choice." She smiled a little, a smile that was beyond my interpretation.

"Alright," I said. "But on one condition."

"What's that?" She stood up and started stacking dishes.

"Actually two conditions," I said.

She stopped what she was doing and looked at me.

I decided to start with the one that was probably going to be easier to sell.

"It'll be late, so you have to let me follow you home."

I saw the indecision and resistance cross her features. Maybe I had chosen the wrong option to start with.

"Okay," she said. "What's the second condition?"

"The second condition is that you sit here on this bar stool and keep me company while I clean this mess up."

I had been right. This was a harder sell.

"Doesn't that rather defeat the purpose?" she asked. "Of me staying?"

"Not for me. I haven't seen you in forever. I wouldn't mind taking a minute to catch up."

I held the stool for her waiting for her to sit down.

She hesitated. Made a face at me, then climbed onto the stool.

"Thank you," I said.

I rolled up my sleeves and gathered everything up to take to the sink.

"How have you been?" I asked as I scraped plates.

"I've been okay," she said.

"So what's up with you and the secret blueprints?"

"I recently took the leap to leave my corporate job and went out on my own. Hence the secret blueprints."

"Wow. Congratulations. That takes a lot of courage." I began filling the dishwasher. "Did you have a lot of jobs lined up ahead of time?"

"Melissa is the first. Actually the second. But the first since I took the leap."

"I'm impressed by your bravery."

"I don't want to wait until I'm older. I want to get a running start at being successful."

I smiled. We had a long way to go before we started to get older, but I understood her way of thinking.

"My brother told me you're on the Skye Travels schedule," she said.

"Your brother? Which one?"

"James."

"James flies for Skye Travels?"

"He does. He swears by Noah Worthington."

"Noah most definitely has the loyalty of his people. I guess I include myself in that group."

"I'd be surprised if you didn't."

I put the last of the dishes in the dishwasher, tossed in a pod, and turned it on.

"There," I said. "That didn't take any time at all."

"You're rather impressive yourself," she said.

"Being single, a man has to learn how to be efficient in keeping things clean."

"We have a housekeeper," she said.

I would have been surprised if she hadn't.

"Ready to get out of here?" I asked.

"Sure," she said. "Do you think they'll notice?"

"I do not. They've got their hands full."

I stopped. Looked at her.

"Unless you want to stay."

"It's late," she said. "I have lots of things to do."

"Okay. Me too."

As we headed out, through the parlor with the gas fireplace burning on low, I had a feeling Melissa had been onto something when she'd suggested that Bella and I stay and hang out.

But the time didn't feel right.

Bella was ready to get home and she was willing to allow me to follow her home.

That was enough.

For now.

Chapter Thirteen

ISABELLA

I pulled out of the Johnson's driveway and followed my GPS out of their neighborhood to the main road. Daniel pulled out right behind me.

The Johnsons lived across town from me. On the other side of the bridges. So I had to drive over the bridge and through the tunnel to get home.

The lights of the city were pretty, but I didn't go out much at night anymore. I had gotten all that out of my system while I was in college.

Now I preferred nice quiet evenings at home. Actually all the Ashtons did, with maybe the exception of my brother Benjamin. Second from the oldest and the middle brother, he did pretty much whatever he wanted to do.

He made it to most of our family dinners in the evenings, but other than that, I rarely saw him.

Hopping onto the highway, I watched my rearview mirror. True to his word, Daniel was right behind me.

I was as independent as the next woman, but I liked having Daniel driving behind me.

It was comforting.

I honestly didn't know what to make of him.

Besides being handsome and sexy, he was a gentleman. He'd let me sit while he did the dishes. After a moment of feeling guilty, I realized that he was making fast work of it. Although I could clean up after myself, it was nice to have someone to do it.

Besides that, he was following me home. I didn't even know where he was staying while he was in Pittsburgh. He'd told Liam and Melissa that he was only here for two months and he was doing a lot of work for his grandmother.

He hardly had time to be following me across town and then back to wherever he was living for his two months.

During dinner I'd caught him looking at me a few times with curiosity and something else. He looked at me with an intensity I couldn't explain.

It reminded me of when we were children and he had kissed me.

It was unlikely that he even remembered that.

That was unfortunate since it was burned into my brain. I couldn't even begin to think how many times I had thought of that day. How many times I'd replayed it in my head.

I told myself it was silly. That we had been children.

And yet I still thought about it.

I had imagined a hundred times what it would be like to see him again.

Seeing him at Melissa and Liam's house had never been on my list of possibilities.

I'd imagined running into him at a coffee shop. Our eyes locking across the room. Maybe even accidentally picking up the other's coffee cup.

Or at a gala. Even better, a masked gala. He'd ask me to dance and we would discover that we knew each other. Maybe after falling in love all over again. We would agree that it was destiny.

Somehow all my imagined reunions with him ended with happily ever after. I didn't judge myself for that. I was, after all, a product of my culture. I loved a good happily ever after. Every year my sister and I watched every Hallmark Christmas movie. It was one of our traditions. So I was well steeped in the concept.

But Daniel.

I didn't know what that was all about. I couldn't explain why he was driving behind me.

I couldn't even explain why it meant so much to me that he was.

I turned off the freeway toward our house. The closer we got, the darker the roads got with fewer street lights.

I'd never been able to explain anything about Daniel.

He had quite simply been Daniel.

He'd always been in my life. We might not have dated, but we had grown up together nonetheless. I'd watched him grow into a man.

He had been the yardstick by which I had measured every other man who came in to my life.

And no one had ever measured up.
Then we went to college and lost touch.
I'd be lying to myself if I said it was by accident.

Chapter Fourteen

DANIEL

A wave of nostalgia washed over me as we turned off the main road and started down the Ashton's mile long driveway. It wasn't really a mile long, but with all the twists and turns through the maple and blue spruce trees, driving at a snail's pace, it seemed like about a mile.

I was quite familiar with this road. My father was best friends with Bella's father and he had come to visit at least once a month, my mother, sister, and me in tow.

Until I turned fourteen.

At fourteen I started hanging out with friends and considered myself too old to go visiting with my family.

Occasionally, when I had nothing better to do, I would go, though, for the simple reason of getting to see Bella.

I never told anyone that I went to see Bella. I was too cool for that.

But Bella had grown up from a pretty little girl into an enchanting teenager to an alluring young woman.

Even though it was late, all the windows of the three-story house were lit up. It was no surprise. Mr. and Mrs. Ashton had raised five children in the old manor house.

Bella still lived here and I didn't know how many of her brothers and sisters still lived at home. Last I'd heard, they all did, but I'd lost touch after my parents moved to Florida and I moved to Houston. My sister lived in California, so she was no help.

If I wanted to keep up with Bella, I should have done it myself.

As she pulled around the circle drive and parked in front of the house, I pulled in behind her and turned off the motor.

"You really didn't have to do this," she said, getting out of her car and slipping into a red leather jacket. The chilly wind swept her hair across her face.

"I know," I said. "But it didn't hurt me to see that you made it home safely."

She started to protest. I saw it in her face.

"Anything could happen. You could have car trouble and end up sitting on the side of the road. It just isn't safe."

"You're right," she said, blowing out a breath and holding her hair back with one hand. "Thank you."

I grinned.

"Now," I said. "Can I walk you to the door?"

"You've always been rather persistent." She started walking toward the door and I went with her.

"Persistence is ninety percent of success, right?" I asked.

"Is it ninety percent?" She looked at me sideways.

"I don't know. I just made that up."

"I hope you're right because persistence is the one thing I have an abundance of."

"Good to know," I said.

She smiled and I couldn't look away. She had the most beautiful smile. It reached all the way to her eyes, lighting up her entire face.

We walked up the steps and stopped when we reached the front door.

"I just installed one of these door locks for my grandmother," I said. "Today, in fact."

"You installed it yourself?"

"I did. And I taught her how to use it. Now she doesn't have to worry about locking herself out."

"That's nice," she said. "I'm impressed that you installed it yourself."

"I'm a handy guy to have around," I said. "If something breaks, I can fix it."

"So you're a pilot and a handyman."

"I consider myself a pilot who can fix things."

She was looking at me, trying to figure something out.

"I can see you thinking," I said.

She laughed. "You can't see me thinking."

I raised a challenging eyebrow.

"Wanna bet?"

"I don't think so," she said, putting a finger against her chin. "But..."

"But?"

"You say you can fix anything?"

"I can fix anything that is man-made."

She crossed her arms and tilted her head to the side.

"Never mind. It's not something that needs to be fixed."

"Try me," I said. "I like a challenge."

"Okay, but promise you won't laugh."

"Cross my heart." I used my fingers to cross my heart.

"I have a desk that they say has a secret compartment, but I can't find it."

"Is that so? That sounds like fun."

"Really? You think so?"

"Absolutely," I said. "I love a challenge. When can I look at it?"

There was that deer in the headlights look again.

"Not tonight," I said quickly. "It's too late. Tomorrow?"

"Sure," she said with obvious relief. "Tomorrow is good."

I grinned. She had given me the perfect excuse to come see her tomorrow. Once I was here, I could work on finding a way to get her to go to dinner with me.

"Give me a goodnight hug," I said, pulling her into a hug.

She fit perfectly against me, her head resting just right beneath my chin. I caught a hint of the scent of charcoal from Liam's grill, but most of all she smelled like jasmine. Jasmine and vanilla with a hint of something that smelled like spruce tree needles after a rain.

Her scent completely caught me off guard.

Beautiful. Funny. Smart. And smelled like an angel.

At heart I was still the same nine-year-old boy enchanted by the pretty girl that I'd wanted to marry.

Only now I was pretty sure that it took more than a kiss to get married.

Chapter Fifteen

ISABELLA

When Daniel pulled me into a hug, I wrapped my arms around his waist and fisted my hands in his shirt.

Resting my cheek against his chest, I closed my eyes.

He smelled like a heady combination of jet fuel and something earthy like pine needles.

I took just a minute.

Just a minute to let myself relax against him. To imagine what it would be like to be able to do this all the time.

Over the years, when I thought about Daniel, sometimes I'd remember that day when he'd taken my hands and kissed me.

It had been an innocent kiss, but it still brought a smile to my lips.

"What are you smiling about?" Daniel asked, running a hand through my hair.

"I'm not smiling," I said, startled.

He pushed back enough that I could see his face in the dim glow of the gas light sconces on either side of the door.

He was the one smiling and I couldn't help but smile back. It was almost reflexive.

"It's good to see you again," he said, tucking a strand of hair behind my ear.

"You too," I said, the words catching in my throat.

I felt like I was spinning.

I had seen Daniel now and then over the years. We'd go for months without seeing each other, then he would just show up with his parents.

We didn't talk, but I'd catch him looking at me, like I had tonight at Liam and Melissa's house.

I'd watched him grow up over the years. He'd been my friend, someone to run and play with, then suddenly when he turned fourteen, it had seemed like he got taller every time I saw him.

Most of what I knew about him, I'd gotten from listening to his parents talk to my parents.

I'd learned that he had lots of girlfriends. Hearing that had broken my heart at first, then I'd just gotten numb to it.

He'd gone to college a year ahead of me. A small local college. Small enough that I'd seen him around. He'd been cordial enough, but he had almost always been with a girl, usually a different girl just about every time.

I'd gone one semester, then I had transferred to a university with an exceptionally strong architectural program.

I'd be lying if I said Daniel hadn't played a part in that decision.

Going to a different college had allowed me to focus on my studies. I'd put my head down. Ran through the undergraduate classes, then went on to get a masters.

My eyes still locked on Daniel's I heard footsteps coming toward the door. The downside of living with one's family of origin was a distinct lack of privacy.

"I'll say goodnight now," Daniel said.

"Goodnight."

When he leaned forward and kissed me on the forehead, my eyes fluttered closed.

"I'll see you tomorrow," he said.

He turned and strode to his car just as someone flipped on the porch light and opened the door.

"Bella?" My sister Charlotte opened the door. She was wearing her pajamas and her hair hung loosely around her shoulders. Charlotte was the kind of sister no one could ever be mad at. She had a good heart and always meant well.

"Are you okay? I saw your car, but you didn't come inside."

"I'm good," I said, stepped out of the wind.

"Who was that?" she asked, spotting the taillights of Daniel's car.

"Just an old friend," I said. "Making sure I got home okay."

"That's sweet," Charlotte said.

"I need to talk to you about something," I said, purposely distracting her from Daniel.

"Now? I'm reading some student papers."

"Tomorrow's fine," I said. "We'll talk tomorrow."

Heading upstairs to my room, I felt a little dreamy. Like a teenager.

I tried to shake off the feeling. A twenty-six year old woman should not be feeling like a schoolgirl over a man she'd had a crush on as a little girl.

But try as I might, the feeling didn't shake off.

Chapter Sixteen

DANIEL

When things started to move, they moved quickly.

I'd gone from having no flights to suddenly having a flight the next day. A Saturday flight.

I had to fly a businessman over to Philadelphia and drop him off.

Fortunately, I wasn't required to wait for him. Someone would pick him up next week. Possibly me.

It didn't matter to me as long as it wasn't today.

Today I had a date with Bella.

Date might be a strong word, but I was claiming it.

Bella had come up with an excuse to get me back to her house without me having to either ask or come up with some harebrained excuse to come back to see her.

Actually figuring out how to open a secret compartment in an old desk sounded like a fun challenge. And figuring it out with Bella... for Bella... made it all the more interesting.

While I waited for my passenger to arrive at the airport, I did a little research on secret compartments in desks. I wasn't trying to cheat. I was just trying to be prepared.

Apparently secret compartments were a thing back in the day— back a couple of centuries ago, especially.

There were so many options. From what I could tell, with the desks being handmade, each one had its own secret compartment. Each one was different.

I wondered how many desks were out there with people's prized possessions hidden away in them. People who had lived hundreds of years ago. Some of the desks, a lot of them, had probably even been destroyed.

It was unfortunate. It would be fascinating to find things people had squirreled away for safekeeping. Things they thought were important enough to hide away from everyone.

I imagined things like money. Or letters. Maybe love letters. Or deeds to property.

Things were different back then. A person couldn't just go to their computer to find a copy of whatever document they were looking for.

The paper document was it.

Those were the thoughts I had as my wheels touched down at the airport back in Pittsburgh.

Bella and I hadn't set a time for me to go by to look at her desk.

Since we hadn't set a time, I figured I could go by anytime.

I also figured that the sooner I got there, the more time I would have to spend with her.

Since my ultimate goal was to get her to go to dinner with me, I didn't want to wait too long.

Going home to shower and change would waste precious time, so I decided against it.

I'd showered before my flight, so I should be okay there.

I'd go straight to her house and save myself at least two hours with all the driving. Maybe more depending on traffic.

No, I decided. It was definitely better to go straight there.

After securing the airplane, I went through the post flight checklist, wrapping things up fairly quickly. It was three thirty by the time I made it to my car.

According to the GPS I would be at Bella's house at four o'clock. Perfect timing. We'd have a couple of hours to fool around with the desk, then I'd segue right into dinner.

I'd let Bella slip out of my hands one time already. I didn't plan on doing it again.

It was funny and kind of sad. I had known what I wanted at nine years old. When I was nine, I had known I wanted to marry Bella Ashton.

Then I had just run from that, going the exact opposite direction.

I'd dated. A lot. But none of them had been Bella.

Not one of them had held a candle to her.

I'd spent all these years searching for the one thing I'd already found.

The very thing I'd had when I was nine-years-old.

I was twenty-seven now and I no longer had an excuse for being young and dumb.

What I wanted had not changed with time.

I just had to figure out how to make it happen.

How did a man court the girl he'd been in love with since he was nine-years-old but hadn't seen in years?

Chapter Seventeen

Isabella

I prowled around the house most of the day.

Daniel hadn't said what time he was coming today to look at my desk. It was an ingenuous, if flimsy, reason for him to come by. I expected him to see right through it. Instead he seemed like it was something he was actually interested in.

After yesterday's winds, the clouds had settled in, making the day a perfectly overcast day.

The fireplace in my third floor studio was gas, but the one downstairs that used wood filled the house with the pleasant cozy scent of fall.

The smell of fresh apple pies our cook was baking today added even more to the cozy feel of the house.

Normally on a day like today, I would have settled in. Gotten a little work done. Maybe settled in with a book for the afternoon.

But instead, I prowled. And I changed clothes three times. I'd started off with casual jeans and an oversized sweater.

Then after lunch, I'd changed into a flowy skirt. I'd rationalized myself into thinking that since Daniel would be coming into my office space, I needed to look somewhat professional.

A couple of hours later, I'd started to feel overdressed for a cloudy Saturday at home, so I'd changed again. I'd put my jeans back on, but this time I put on a black cashmere sweater set.

With it nearing three thirty, I took my book downstairs and curled up on the big comfortable sectional.

Everyone else was doing their own thing, so I had it to myself.

I read a paragraph. Then read it again.

Maybe Daniel had changed his mind. Maybe since we hadn't set a time he hadn't thought he was really supposed to come. Maybe he had a date.

With a frustrated sigh, I forced myself to read all the way through a chapter.

He was probably tied up with his grandmother. According to what he told Liam, he was doing some major work on her house.

If Daniel didn't come, it was okay.

I would have dinner with whoever in my family didn't go out. I'd go to bed early. Get some much needed rest. Then tomorrow I would get up early and finish up the changes on Melissa's office cottage.

It was a good plan, I decided.

Then I heard a car pull up and stop in front of the house.

My heart pounding much too quickly, I got up and went to the front window.

It was Daniel.

I straightened my sweater. Ran a hand through my hair.

Then squared my shoulders and tried to look easy and casual. I needed to answer the door with a friendly, welcoming smile.

Friendly and welcoming. And casual.

Nearly forgot he was coming by today.

Standing back, I waited for him to knock on the door.

The tall grandfather clock in the foyer chimed four times.

When I opened the door I was pretty sure my friendly and casual changed into something a bit more intense.

He was wearing his pilot's uniform. Dark pants and matching blazer. A white button down shirt and a red tie. Same uniform my brother who worked for Skye Travels wore.

But Daniel wore his uniform a whole lot differently than my brother. Better. Sooo much better.

He removed the sun glasses he didn't need on such a cloudy day and smiled.

"Hi," he said.

"Hi." I stepped back to let him inside.

"I hope it's not too late," he said. "I just got back from a flight to Philadelphia."

So not a date and not his grandmother. It hadn't even occurred to me that he might be working.

"It's not too late," I said. "I was just doing some reading." I shoved my hands in my back pockets. "How was your flight?"

"It was uneventful."

"The best kind, right?"

"You know it." He grinned. "It smells good in here."

"Cook made an apple pie."

"That sounds good."

"Do you want some?" I asked.

"Sure. I'll eat some with you."

I raised an eyebrow at him. "You trying to score me an extra mile on the treadmill?"

He laughed.

"How about if we split it?"

"Okay," I said. "We can split it."

Was it possible that he was just here to hang out?

It occurred to me then that he might be here to see my brother.

"James isn't home," I said as we walked past the parlor into the kitchen.

"Okay. He's married, right?"

"Yes."

"Good for him."

Two pies were sitting in the middle of the kitchen island. Cook was nowhere to be seen.

"Have a seat," I said, going to the cabinet to get a couple of plates and a knife.

"Is this going to get us in trouble?" he asked.

"Trouble how?" I asked, sitting down and holding up the knife over one of the pies.

"Maybe Cook made these for a someone. You know. An occasion."

"This is an occasion," I said, slicing the knife into the still hot apple pie.

He smiled and watched as I slid a piece of pie onto a plate. Handed him a fork.

He cut off a piece and held it out.

I looked at him questioningly.

"We're splitting it, right?"

I smiled and let him feed me the bite of pie.

The pie was good, but I barely tasted it.

I was in so much trouble and not from the pie.

It was Daniel. My heart was definitely in trouble with Daniel.

Chapter Eighteen

DANIEL

Bella had a nice view from her third floor studio. A big lawn that ended at the edge of the forest. The lawn was scattered with maple trees, aglow with bright red leaves, and blue spruce trees that had grown up since I'd been here last.

It was nice. Nothing like the view from my twenty-first floor apartment. It was just a small one bedroom, but what could I say? I liked being in the air. It was a pilot thing.

"You've got a nice studio set up here," I said. "I like the way your drafting table is in front of the window to catch the natural light."

"I like it," she said. "So much better than working in a cubicle."

"I can't even imagine having to do that." I turned around. "Is this the desk we talked about?"

The old desk was obviously heavy from back when furniture had weight—built out of real wood.

It was old, but well taken care of. Big. With lots of drawers and, I soon discovered, it was a roll top desk.

The vase of fresh daffodils sitting on the top of the desk filled the room with a sweet, fresh scent.

"I have a feeling this isn't going to be easy," I said.

"Trust me," she said. "It's not. I've been all over it."

"And no one has found it yet? How do you know it has a secret compartment?"

I ran a hand over the light oak wood.

"My grandmother told me. I got the desk from her."

"A lady's desk," I said. "Of course it has secrets."

"Funny," she said. "But probably true. I emptied it. Moved everything out of the drawers."

"Where do you suggest we start?"

"I don't know." She pulled down the roll top, then slid it back up. "It's all in good shape."

"It's in excellent shape. Obviously well cared for."

"You know about antiques?"

"Not really." I opened up one of the drawers. "When my parents moved to Florida, they didn't want to take anything with them. So I kept a couple of pieces. Sentimental reasons. My grandmother has the rest."

A dog barked outside. I glanced out the window, saw a black lab racing around the yard.

"My sister-in-law's dog," she said. "That must be so strange to have your family scattered like that."

"I guess I've gotten used to it."

"So what do you think?" she asked. "Do you think you can find the secret compartment?"

I rubbed my hands together. "Only one way to find out."

She sat down in her office chair.

"Oh no," I said. "We're doing this together."

"I've looked everywhere," she said.

"But you haven't looked with me."

I locked my gaze onto her green siren eyes and smiled.

This was going to be fun.

Besides, there was a magic that happened when two people looked together.

I wouldn't tell her that, though. Not yet anyway.

Chapter Nineteen

Isabella

Having Daniel in my studio felt surreal.

He made the space seem smaller somehow.

I'd put all my pencils and rulers and other supplies in a box so that he wouldn't have to worry about going through my things.

Biscuit was barking out back. Probably saw a deer at the edge of the woods. He wouldn't go into the woods by himself. Not sure who taught him that or if he was just a super smart dog, but bears had been sighted out there in the woods.

Bears and pets did not mix well.

Daniel wanted me to help him look through the desk, but I'd already been through the whole thing.

"I don't think I'm going to be any help," I said. "I really have looked through the whole thing."

"It's different when two people look together," he said.

"Okay."

I went to kneel next to him in front of the desk.

"Most people start at the top," I said.

He looked at me sideways with those deep blue eyes of his that reminded me of a clear summer day.

"Exactly," he said and pulled out the bottom drawer. He ran his hands over it, turned it over and examined the bottom, then handed it over to me.

"You're very thorough."

He took out his phone, turned on the flashlight, and looked into the space where the drawer was.

"Do you see anything?" I asked.

"Not yet." He sat back on his heels. "I think we should take the whole thing apart. All the drawers out. And go from there."

"Okay," I said. "I didn't do that."

"We have a plan then."

One by one, he pulled out each drawer, examined it, then handed it over to me.

I lined them up, keeping them in order.

He and I were a lot alike, I realized. Both very methodical.

As a pilot, he would have to be. Same for me as an architect.

Both of us had to be precise in what we did.

With the desk apart, he sat back and examined it.

He looked over at me, a satisfied look in his eyes.

"I think I know where it is."

"No way. There's no way you could know already."

"Look." He pointed to a drawer space in the middle on the left side.

"This one doesn't go as far back as the other ones."

I leaned over close to him.

He smelled good. Like pine needles and jet fuel.

I'd never known that jet fuel was an attractive scent. Maybe someone should capture the scent and make a man's cologne out of it.

I forced myself to focus on what he was showing me.

"You're right."

I leaned forward, looked into the space, then looked back at him.

"You're good."

"Let's not count our chickens," he said.

"How do we get back there?"

"I don't quite know yet. I don't want to break anything."

"If it's a secret compartment, there has to be a way in without breaking it."

"Good point."

He ducked beneath center of the desk and ran his hands along the wood.

"We need to look behind it," he said, standing up.

"You can't move... it—" I stopped in mid-sentence as he slid the desk out. "It's too heavy."

Back on his knees again, he checked the back wall of the desk.

"Doesn't look like anyone's cut into it," I said, looking over his shoulder.

"Like you said. There has to be a way without all that."

With the desk back in place, we knelt side by side and considered the space.

Then he looked at me.

"I can see you thinking," I said.

He looked at me and laughing, nudged my arm with his. "I win the bet."

"I concede that point," I said. "We need to take a break away from it. We'll figure it out."

"Good idea," I said.

He stood up and held out a hand. I put my hand in his and let him pull me to my feet.

"Just need a shower," I said to myself.

"Oh." He sniffed his sleeve. "I need a shower?"

"No," I said. "I just meant." I put a hand over my mouth to keep from laughing, but it didn't help. I couldn't keep from laughing.

"What?"

"I'm sorry," I said, biting my lip and trying to look serious. "It's just." I couldn't even talk, I was trying so hard not to laugh.

"Do I need to run home? Shower?"

I cleared my throat.

"I just meant that I do my best thinking in the shower." I had to say it quickly because I was laughing again.

He simply watched me with amusement.

"Actually I'm the same way," he said. "If you think we should go shower, I'm on board."

I stopped laughing and just looked at him.

Had Daniel Benton just suggested that we shower? Together?

It was like being slapped in the face with a rude reminder that Daniel was a player. No one had specifically called him that, but I just had a feeling.

Chapter Twenty

Daniel

After watching Bella laugh like a loon, which I found perfectly enchanting by the way, she suddenly grew serious and withdrawn.

I'd only been teasing her about taking a shower. She'd been the one to bring it up.

Not that I would complain.

We went back down to the kitchen for a drink.

"Where is everybody?" I asked.

"I don't really know," she said. "It's a big house. My grandparents and parents are out of town. I don't know about everyone else."

"How many of your siblings still live here?"

"All of them. And both Henry and James are married now. So we have two more people living here."

"Wow. That's a lot."

"As you can see," she said. "It's not a big deal. I get to live in a nice big house. No rent. And it often feels like I have it to myself."

I nodded. "That is different."

"And then there are times when it seems like there are a hundred people here. Do you want a beer?" she asked.

"Whatever you have."

"I have everything."

"Then I'll have whatever you're having."

"Wine then," she said, going over to the wine cooler and selecting a bottle of wine.

Another way that our worlds were different. She not only lived in a big house with her big family, but she had a ready selection of wine to choose from.

If I were in her shoes, I'd probably never leave home either.

After opening the wine, she handed me a glass and kept one for herself.

"This is good wine," I said, following her to the parlor.

There was a fire going. A fire with wood that was burning low.

"Hold my glass," I said, not knowing where to set it. "And I'll get this fire going."

Minutes later, I had the fire going again using the wood stacked neatly next to the fireplace.

"You're handy," she said, handing me my glass of wine as I sat next to her on the big oversized sectional sofa. The sofa fit the room and I could see where it could be a gathering place for the family.

"Is this yours?" I asked, picking up a book on the sofa.

"Yes," she said.

"I've read some of her others, but I haven't read this one."

She looked at me suspiciously. "You don't read romantasy."

"I certainly do," I said. "I read the one before this where they went to Galveston and stayed in a haunted house. There was a ghost named... Ophelia."

She blinked and took another sip of her wine.

"Another point conceded."

"I'm not sure what I'm going to get with all these points," I said. "But I'm winning all over the place."

"You're very funny," she said. "Very funny."

"So what do you think is in the desk?"

"I don't know."

"Come on," I said. "You read good fiction. Surely you have some ideas."

"Letters," she said.

"That's what I'm thinking. Has to be letters."

I looked up when someone came to the door.

"Daniel? Is that you?"

"Hey. James." I stood up. Shook his hand.

"I saw your name on the flight schedule."

I hadn't seen James in years. He looked good. Fit. And happy.

"Yeah. Noah needed me to cover for a couple of months."

"Right." James glanced over at Bella. Then back to me. "Good to see you."

"You too."

"So Tori and I are going out to dinner," he said to Bella. "I was just gonna see if you wanted anything."

"No," Bella said. "I think we're good."

"Okay. Well. Call if you change your mind. Happy to bring you something."

"Have fun."

"See you later Daniel."

"Sure thing."

I watched James walk off, waited until I heard the back door close.

"Were you supposed to go with them?" I asked.

"Not invited," I said.

"Huh."

"Newlyweds."

"I see."

It suddenly occurred to me with something of a jolt that being part of a big family didn't mean a person wasn't lonely.

That Bella didn't even expect to be invited out to dinner with her brother and his wife made me sad for her. Sad for her and a little disappointed in James.

I knew enough about family dynamics, though, to know that things weren't always as they seemed. It was quite possible that Bella wouldn't want to go to dinner with her brother and his wife. It was the kind of thing a man had to leave alone.

Feeling even more determined to make sure she had a good evening I sat back down next to Bella.

"Do you have plans for dinner?" I asked.

Sometimes a guy had to just jump right out there.

Chapter Twenty-One

ISABELLA

Sitting next to Daniel in front of the cozy fire with a glass of wine was unexpected.

He didn't seem to be in any hurry to leave.

I'd expected him to just take a look at the desk, look for the secret compartment, then leave.

But he was still here.

My brother James seemed surprised to see him here. With me.

It almost looked like they were sizing each other up. James was somewhere around ten years older than Daniel, so they never really knew each other very well.

Maybe James thought Daniel was trying to date me. Getting the cart before the horse on that.

I couldn't really say why he was here.

Maybe he was just being friendly. Reminiscing since he remembered us from when he grew up here in Pittsburgh and used to come here with his family to visit.

I realized I was driving myself a little bit crazy trying to figure out why he was here.

I should just enjoy the moment and not try so hard to figure it out. There didn't have to be an explanation. He could just be here to hang out.

A couple of friends from the old days.

"I don't have plans for dinner," I said.

"Want to go out? Get something?"

That was not anything near what I'd been expecting for today. At most, I'd thought maybe he would stay for dinner. Eat with the family if any of them were around. There was always someone around so it wasn't like we'd be alone.

But going out? That was different.

"Okay," I said. "Sure."

Since he didn't appear to be in any hurry to leave, I sat back, sipped my wine.

"This is nice," he said.

"It's a lot different from where you live in Houston, I bet."

"A different world." He gave his head a little shake. "I know Pittsburgh is a city and it's right there, but it doesn't feel like we're in the city. Not out here."

"I know."

"You like living in Houston?" I asked, then instantly regretted asking. It sounded like a leading question, but I hadn't intended it that way. I really had just been curious.

"I do," he said, swirling the burgundy wine in his glass. "I'm not home very much, but when I am I have an apartment on the twenty-first floor."

I laughed. "You like being in the air, huh?"

"I guess I do. It's a pilot thing."

"I'm quite familiar with that phenomenon," I said. "Two brothers as pilots and all."

"Yes. I'm sure you are. But they don't seem to mind living here."

"I guess it's because we're a close family."

"Yeah." He looked into the fire.

"I'm sorry," I said. "I know you must miss yours."

"It's okay. Everyone seems to be happy where they are."

"Your parents are in Florida. Your grandmother is here. You're in Houston. And where is your sister?"

"California."

"Wow. You definitely have the country covered." Using a finger, I drew a box of sorts in the air.

"Wait," Daniel said. "That's it."

"What's it?"

"The desk." He stood up. Held out a hand to help me up. "I think I just figured it out."

"Really?" On our feet now, we headed back upstairs to my third floor studio.

Hands on his hips, he looked at the drawers I had lined up.

"Which one goes with the secret compartment?"

I picked up one of the drawers.

"This one."

Getting back on his knees, he slid the drawer into its space.

"Now what?" I asked, kneeling next to him.

He ran a hand along the edges of it, then he pushed hard.

The drawer went in an inch, then popped back out. When he slid the drawer back out, the faux wall was gone.

"How did you? What? I don't underst—"

"I got lucky," he said, grinning.

"What's in there?"

He pulled out a stack of letters neatly tied with a white ribbon.

"You were right," he said. "Letters."

"Guess I got lucky, too."

He set the letters down between us. We just looked at them.

"Is it just me or does it seem wrong to read someone's letters?"

"It's not just you," he said. "But these are really old."

He looked into my eyes.

"If we don't read them, who will?"

"You make a good point."

I picked them up.

"There are a lot of letters here. We should take them downstairs."

"Dinner first?" he asked, "Then we can read someone's love letters."

"What makes you think they're love letters?" I asked.

"Why else would someone keep letters like this?" he asked.

I could think of a few reasons, but I kept them to myself. I liked the idea of the love letters a whole lot more than anything else I could think of.

Chapter Twenty-Two

DANIEL

I took Bella to an Italian place on the river someone had told me about. It was new to me and didn't look like it had been here very long.

It was loud and it was crowded.

It was perfect.

There was nothing better than a loud crowded restaurant to create an intimate, cozy environment.

The music and voices were loud. We couldn't hear each other without leaning close.

And since there was a wait list, we started out in the bar.

I'd had my quota of wine at Bella's house, so I ordered a seltzer. She ordered a martini with extra olives.

We found two empty stools side by side at the bar and settled in.

"Have you been here before?" I asked.

"No."

Bella had changed into a skirt and some black boots that zipped up the sides.

She'd only taken thirty minutes to get ready, but she'd not only changed from jeans to a skirt, she had also done something with her hair.

It was straighter and had some curl in it at the same time.

It took all the effort I could muster to keep my eyes on hers and not watch the lips she'd smeared some sexy pink gloss on.

I wasn't sure what we'd call this if we had to call it something, but I'd say she was dressed for a date.

Definitely the prettiest girl in the restaurant.

"So," I said. "What was it like to find out that Noah Worthington is your uncle?"

"You know about that?" she asked, sliding an olive off her toothpick with her lips.

"Yeah. I heard about it. I was working for Noah when your grandfather had his heart attack."

"That was a scary time. There was a lot going on back then."

"How is he now?" I asked. "Your grandfather?"

"He's doing well. He and Grandma are traveling a lot."

"That's why I didn't see them," I said.

"Yeah. The house is too quiet without them."

My phone vibrated in my pocket.

"Our table is ready."

I held the bar stool while she slid off, then after tucking her hand over my arm, grabbed our drinks and followed the hostess to a table in the back of the restaurant.

We sat across from each other, then after the hostess left, I got up to shift chairs and sat next to her.

"Too far away," I said. "Can't hear each other."

She just smiled.

During dinner we talked about everything and nothing. Mostly we caught each other up on what we'd been doing for the last few years. I told her about some of the places I'd flown and she told me about how she'd finally taken the leap to go into business for herself.

It was nearly two hours later when we finally left the table and made our way toward the front door.

I requested my car from the valet, then we waited inside out of the wind.

"Winter's coming fast this year," she said.

"I'm definitely not used to the cold anymore," I said.

"Isabella? Hey!" A young man, about our age came up to Bella and gave her a hug.

"George," she said. "Hi. How are you?"

"Okay," he said, glancing at me. "We miss you at work."

"Daniel," she said. "This is George from where I used to work."

"Good to meet you." I shook hands with George.

He was cordial, but it was clear that he was interested in Bella.

"Our car's here," I said as the valet pulled up with my car.

"Good to see you," Bella said. "Tell everyone I said hi."

After we were settled in the car and I pulled out onto the main road, I looked over at Bella.

"Your friend George likes you."

"George?" She made a face. "He just likes to have help on his projects."

"You worked on projects together?"

"A few."

"You dated him?" I asked, going with my philosophy of just jumping out there if I wanted to know something.

"George? No. Not my type."

"No? What's your type?"

She was quiet for a minute.

"I don't think I have a type," she said finally.

I wanted to ask how she knew George wasn't her type if she didn't have one, but I didn't. I decided to let it slide. To save this conversation for another day.

Chapter Twenty-Three

ISABELLA

I was quiet on the drive home.

The lights of Pittsburgh were beautiful at night.

We had to cross the main bridge across the river, then drive through the tunnel.

Daniel had me thinking too much.

I knew who my type guy was, but I couldn't tell him.

It wouldn't be proper.

I couldn't tell him that he was my type.

Always had been.

Since that day he'd taken my hands, kissed me, and declared us married.

We'd only been children, but that moment had branded itself on my brain.

Somewhere deep in the recesses of my mind, I think I had always —on some primal level—considered myself married to him.

I'd never told anyone about it and he and I had never spoken of it again.

But it was there.

My first marriage proposal at age nine.

Actually my only marriage proposal.

I hadn't exactly put myself out there.

I was the complete opposite of Daniel.

He had dated all the girls and I had dated only a handful of guys.

And even with the handful of guys I'd dated, my heart hadn't been in it.

I'd always compared them to Daniel. Even after I went off to college and didn't see him anymore, I still compared other men to him.

And now that I had seen him again... spent time with him again... other men didn't stand a chance.

It was probably a little odd to crush on the same guy for almost all of one's life, but there were worse things. There were most definitely worse things.

The thing that made it bad was that after he had "married" me, he had continued to date.

I never held it against him.

When I was younger I didn't even understand any of it.

After that, I had no explanation. It was just the way it was.

"I kept you out late," he said as he drove down our long winding driveway beneath the maples and oaks and blue spruce trees.

"You did," I said with a little smile. "Do you have a flight tomorrow?"

"Not that I know of. But as you know, it just takes one phone call to change that."

"I'm well-versed in the life of a pilot."

He pulled up, around the circle drive, and parked in front of the door.

"I was thinking," he said. "Are you willing to wait until tomorrow to read the letters we found in the desk?"

"Sounds like a good way to spend a Sunday afternoon," I said.

And it also sounded like a good excuse, intentional on his part or not, to get to see him again.

"I'll come around," he said, unhooking his seatbelt. "Walk you to the door."

As I waited for Daniel to come around, it occurred to me that there weren't very many gentlemen out there or if there were, then I hadn't dated them.

He opened the passenger door and held it while I got out.

The moon had settled behind the clouds, leaving the night dark and chilly. The darkness was broken only by the pale glow flickering from the gas lamps on either side of the front door.

"You've got to make me a promise," he said.

I had a flashback to standing beneath a maple tree in my back-yard, hungry little birds calling for food. Daniel gripping my hands. His lips touching mine.

Declaring us married.

Forever and ever.

"What kind of promise?" I asked, reaching the front door.

"Don't go reading those letters without me," he said.

I don't know what I'd been expecting. Something more dramatic.

"Don't worry," I said. "I'm going straight to sleep."

He took my hand. Kissed the back of it.

"I'll see you tomorrow," he said.

I keyed in my code to open the door, but instead of going right inside, I stood and watched Daniel drive off. I watched until his tail-lights vanished around the curve in the trees.

I might be going straight up to bed, but I wasn't so sure just how much sleep I'm was going to get.

A kiss on the hand was still a kiss. Right?

Chapter Twenty-Four

DANIEL

"Which color do you like?" I asked, stepping back so that my grandmother could see the three paint swatches I had brushed on the pale gray wall.

I'd picked a spot in the breakfast nook that had the best morning sunlight. Slid the table aside and spread a tarp on the floor.

One swatch was a light blue—sky blue. One was a neutral cream color. And the other was a sage green.

Somehow the sage green reminded me of Bella's eyes.

My grandmother stood next to me. She was wearing a pair of dark gray slacks and a light gray sweater.

"I like the green," she said.

"Yeah? Me too." Though I was certain we liked the green for different reasons. "You going somewhere?" I asked. "You look nice."

"Thank you," she said, running a hand down her slacks. She was looking a little uncharacteristically nervous.

"Meeting your friend for brunch?" I asked. It was too late for breakfast and too early for lunch.

"Brunch, yes," she said.

"I'm thinking we'll paint this area green and use the cream color in the kitchen."

"You always did have a good eye," she said, fussing with her hair a bit.

"You okay?" I asked. "You're looking a bit nervous."

"Oh no," she said. "I'm okay." She sat down and watched me gather up the three brushes for cleaning. "But I'm not having brunch with Bea."

"No?" I looked up at her over my shoulder. "Who with?"

"Just a fellow I met at book club."

"A man?" I sat back on my heels and looked at my grandmother.

It had never occurred to me that she might want to go on a date. It should have. She was an attractive widow. There was no reason why she wouldn't want to date.

"Yes," she said. "I know it's silly. I'm too old to be thinking about going out with a man."

"Grandma," I said. "You are never too old to go on a date."

"You don't think so?" She smiled. I'd also never thought that she might want my blessing.

"Absolutely," I said. "You should go and have a good time."

She nodded. "I will. Thank you."

"Grandma," I said. "You know you don't have to marry someone just because you go on a date with them."

Grandma looked at me sideways.

"It sounds to me like you're talking from experience."

I laughed.

"Yes ma'am. I might be."

My grandmother was the only person I'd told about that day when I'd married Bella beneath the maple trees.

I'd been so excited about it. So happy.

But Grandma had explained to me that I was too young to get married and that a kiss did not make two people married.

I had moped around for days after that. I'd been so excited to be married to Bella only to find out that there were other things involved.

In her defense, I remembered what else she told me. "Just wait until you're older. Then you can marry her for real if you still want to."

Looking back I think she had unintentionally changed the way I thought.

I'd only been a child. The words "if you still want to" had inadvertently struck a discordant chord with me. At the tender age of nine, I had thought wanting to be married to someone meant wanting to be married to her forever.

If that changed. If there was a possibility that I might not want to be married to her when I was older, then I was very confused about my feelings and what it meant to be married.

Grandma and Grandpa were happily married and had been my whole life. It was just the way it was.

I checked my watch. If Grandma was going out, then I would grab something to eat, stop by my apartment to change clothes, then head out to Bella's house.

I had some things I needed to clarify for myself. Some unresolved issues from that day when I was nine years old.

Chapter Twenty-Five

ISABELLA

Just as I had predicted, I'd had some trouble sleeping.

I couldn't stop thinking about Daniel.

I replayed parts of our conversations.

I even imagined what it would be like to date him.

But every time I got very far, past last night, I hit a mental road block.

He would be going back to Houston. He was only here in Pittsburgh for two months. It was less than two months now.

Time was moving too quickly.

I wanted to slow time down.

It was after nine o'clock in the morning when I woke up.

It startled me a little because I never slept this late.

But I gave myself a pass. It was Sunday and I'd had a date with

Daniel last night.

Not only that, but he was coming over today, too.

Excitement humming through me, I jumped into the shower and let the hot water wash away any lingering sleepiness.

Today Daniel and I would read the love letters we'd found hidden away in the desk. The more I thought about it, the more I was convinced that Daniel was right.

They had to be love letters.

He'd called it a lady's desk. A lady would have hidden the letters away. They could be from her husband or maybe even from a secret lover.

The letters could be hundreds of years old.

We'd sit in front of the fireplace and read through them.

Thinking about spending the afternoon curled up in front of the fireplace with Daniel, no matter what we did, letters or no letters, sent tingly chills along my spine.

I could barely believe my good luck in running into Daniel. If I hadn't gotten the request to design an office cottage for Liam, then he would have come and gone and I wouldn't even have known it.

It seemed like fate had brought us back together.

I was having a hard time believing that it was just coincidence. The odds of it all coming together like it had were too astronomical to calculate.

I believed that we were meant to be reacquainted if for no other reason than for unresolved issues.

I'd spent far too much time thinking about Daniel over the years. I'd compared other men to him.

And that's how I was still single at twenty-six.

Maybe I would find out that he wasn't so perfect after all and I could move on to date other guys after he went back to Houston.

Standing in my closet contemplating what I should wear today, I realized that thought wasn't sitting well with me. Not at all.

It was actually giving me a headache.

I didn't want to move on from Daniel. That wasn't what I wanted to do at all.

I wanted us to figure out a way to be together.

I was a hopeless case, I decided as I yanked a sweatshirt off a hanger.

Today I was going to dress casually. Jeans and a sweatshirt. Just to prove to myself that I knew better than to put too much hope into Daniel.

He was here temporarily.

We weren't nine years old anymore.

And he wasn't here to start anything.

Chapter Twenty-Six

DANIEL

I went ahead and put a first coat of sage green paint on my grandmother's breakfast nook wall just to see how it was going to look.

It looked refreshed. It was a good thing to do for her. A fresh coat of paint could make her feel proud to have people over. Even a beau.

It was cute to watch my grandmother head out looking nervous for her brunch date.

I didn't want her to get hurt. That was the only thing about her dating.

When people started dating they often got hurt for one reason or another.

But it was worth the risk to find someone companionable.

Companionship would be what she was looking for at her age.

Hopefully her date would go well and she would have a bit of happiness in her life.

As I carefully painted one of the corners, I realized that I hadn't enjoyed dating in a really long time. It had just been something I had done.

Going through the motions. Not looking for anything serious.

In all my dating, I hadn't found anyone that I wanted to get serious with. I'd broken a few hearts, but I knew they would get over it and find someone who was right for them. Then they would thank me.

But with Bella, it was different.

I was actually looking forward to spending time with her.

In fact, I couldn't stop thinking about her.

With the first coat of paint finished, I cleaned up and headed to my apartment to shower and change clothes.

I didn't know what I was going to do about Bella just yet. Our options, actually, were limited.

Moving back to Pittsburgh wasn't on my agenda and leaving Pittsburgh wasn't on hers.

We could only take this relationship so far.

Suddenly in a foul mood, I locked up Grandma's house and made the drive over to my temporary apartment.

I was starting to think of it as home. I had to remind myself that it was not home. The apartment belonged to Noah Worthington.

I would be back in Houston in time for Christmas.

And my time with Bella would be behind me.

After a quick shower to get the paint off, I tugged on a pair of jeans and put on a comfortable sweatshirt over a t-shirt.

We would spend the afternoon reading old letters. No need to be uncomfortable for that.

I had to be careful not to lead Bella into thinking we could be something we couldn't.

Logistically, we were bound apart.

It was ironic because I usually embraced distance. I'd used the distance excuse countless times to end relationships.

And now the one time that I did not want it to end, it was going to end for the very excuse that I had relied upon countless times.

Maybe it was Karma.

Or maybe it was just real life.

The reality of being a pilot was that I didn't stay in one place for very long, except of course, Houston. The city I had chosen to live and work.

If Bella lived in Houston, everything would be different.

I had today.

So that's what I would take.

I would take today and make the most of it.

After today we would see.

After today perhaps everything could go back to normal.

I would spend some time with Bella.

And perhaps my emotional ties to her would lessen some.

Chapter Twenty-Seven

ISABELLA

Before lunch I got some work done on Melissa and Liam's office cottage.

I incorporated the changes Melissa requested and was feeling pretty good about it all. My next task was to put everything into the computer program to have it ready for the contractor.

I wouldn't do that though until Melissa approved the plans and all the paperwork was finalized.

It was one of those rare weekends when both my grandparents and parents weren't home. Without them here, my siblings all went to friends' houses for lunch leaving me alone in the house.

Very rare.

About one thirty I went into the kitchen and made myself an

egg sandwich. Biscuit watched me with soulful puppy dog eyes so I made him an egg, too.

"Don't tell your mother," I told him. "No need to get me in trouble like that."

He lapped it up like he was starving before I even sat down at the breakfast table with my own sandwich.

He laid down at my feet, his head on his front paws.

Maybe dogs weren't so bad.

As I ate, I watched a couple of deer frolicking across the lawn below the maple trees. The bright red leaves fell like rain from their limbs.

With such a large family, someone always around, I rarely felt lonely. But now, sitting here by myself with no one to keep me company other than Biscuit, I realized that if it weren't for my family, I wouldn't live here.

I'd live in a more urban environment like I had when I had gone to college. Just because I didn't go out much didn't mean I didn't appreciate the urban environment.

I was still reflecting on that when I heard a car door slam out front.

Quickly putting away my plate, I made a quick stop by the half bath to check my hair, then went to the door.

Seeing Daniel walking across the veranda was a surreal feeling. He walked quickly with purpose.

Today he was wearing blue jeans and a sweatshirt. Dressed much like I was. We were on the same wavelength today, it seemed.

"Hi," I said, opening the door.

"Hi." He looked down. "Who's that?"

Biscuit, having followed me to the door, sat at my feet.

"Oh. This is Biscuit. James and Tori's dog."

"Hi Biscuit," he said.

Biscuit barked once.

Daniel scratched him behind the ears.

"Do you have a dog?" I asked as we went inside.

"No. Wouldn't be fair to him. I'm hardly ever home."

"Right." I knew that, of course. For just a moment I had chosen to forget it. I'd chosen not think of Daniel as always being away from home.

It was just another reminder of how different our lives were. I worked from home and he was hardly ever home.

"Can I get you something?" I asked. "Something to drink? Are you hungry?"

"I ate a little something," he said, Biscuit following along at his heels. "Maybe some apple pie later if you still have any."

"Sure," I said. "There might be some left unless my brothers got into it."

"It's quiet today," he said as we stepped into the parlor.

"Oddly enough," I said. "No one's here at the moment."

He stopped and looked at me. "That's got to be unusual."

"Very."

We sat next to each other on the big sectional and looked at the neatly tied stack of letters on the coffee table in front of us.

Biscuit curled up on the rug in front of the fire, simmering low.

"Want me to get the fire going?" he asked.

I wasn't sure if he was asking me or Biscuit. I decided I had to be the one to answer.

"Sure. Are you stalling?" I asked.

"About the letters?" He went to kneel in front of the fireplace next to Biscuit. Tossed a log onto the fire." Maybe a little. Right now the letters could be anything."

"Sort of like Schrodinger's cat," I said, picking up the stack of letters and placing them in my lap.

"Sort of," he said, poking at the logs with the iron poker. "Except a whole lot less complicated."

Toying with the silk ribbon someone had tied neatly into a bow possibly centuries ago, I realized that Daniel being here was like Schrodinger's cat.

Neither one of us knew what was going to happen. He and I could simply have this quiet Sunday afternoon together and that would be that.

Or yet there was a possibility, however remote, that we might be on the edge of something much more meaningful.

Maybe even possibly a continuation of what we started when we were nine years old.

Except that we had no way of knowing.

Not until we opened the box and looked.

Chapter Twenty-Eight

DANIEL

Kneeling in front of the fire, next to the big black oversized puppy, I acknowledged that Bella was right.

I was stalling.

It wasn't the letters, exactly. Not the letters themselves.

It was the act of reading the letters.

With Bella.

I was here because the letters were the reason for my being here.

We'd read the letters.

Then my excuse for being here would be over.

It was a little unexpected that I'd thrown on jeans and a sweatshirt and that she had done the same.

She looked a lot cuter in hers, though, than I did. Carnegie

Mellon University. A clear reminder that she had split off and gone somewhere different than I did.

It was a good university for architecture, so I had to assume that was her reasoning. Assumptions, though, were dangerous.

Her hair back in a messy ponytail, she sat on the sofa with the letters in her lap.

Satisfied with the fire, I went to sit next to her.

There was only one solution I could see to the problem at hand.

I needed to find another excuse for hanging out with her.

She looked at me with her green siren eyes, luring me over the rocks toward her.

I would find another reason for being here.

Actually she was giving me a reason right now and she didn't even know it.

Her deadly green eyes called to me.

I was a man besotted.

I was a nine year old boy again. Standing beneath a maple tree. Instead of birds chirping, a fire crackled in the background.

I'd wanted to kiss her then and I wanted to kiss her now.

"What?" she asked, biting her lip with a little smile.

But not now. Too soon.

"Nothing," I said. "I was just thinking."

She nodded and slowly untied the ribbon.

"I took a picture of it," she said. "So we have proof. You know. Just in case this turns out to be something really important."

"Like state secrets?"

"Something like that."

"Should I record the process?"

"I don't know," she said.

"I can see you thinking again."

She smiled. "What's the saying?"

"When in doubt, err on the side of caution."

"Why don't we just snap some photos?"

"Sounds good to me. I have a feeling these letters were far more important to the young lady who hid them away than to anyone else."

"You're probably right," she said. "And I think you're right. I think they belonged to a girl, but..." She ran a hand along the first letter. "This looks like a man's handwriting."

"Let's take a look."

She turned over the first letter.

"It's still sealed."

"Let me see."

I took the letter. It felt old. Really old. I handled it carefully so as not to tear it.

I put a finger beneath the seal and it crumbled.

"It's really old," I said, unfolding the parchment, brown with age.

"What does it say?" she asked leaning close.

June 3, 1861.

My Dearest Abigail,

I am writing this with a heavy heart.

I feel that this war is going to last longer, much longer than everyone thought. It could last for years.

A moment doesn't pass when I don't think of you.

I miss you more than you could ever know.

Your love,
Benjamin

Bella flipped through the letters.

"There are dozens of these letters here." She looked at me, her eyes moist with unshed tears. "None of them were ever opened."

"Do you recognize the names? Abigail? Or Benjamin?"

"No," she said. "It was so long ago. During the Civil War."

"Yeah." I refolded the letter and handed it back to her.

"I'm not sure I have the heart to read these."

"I know." I ran a hand through my hair. I hated seeing that sad expression in her eyes. "It might be a good time to check for that apple pie."

Chapter Twenty-Nine

Isabella

"Who named you Biscuit anyway?" Daniel asked the dog as I got out the apple pie.

Biscuit barked twice.

"Do you think he said Mama or Daddy?" Daniel asked.

"I don't know. It could be either of them. You know, I was thinking if I had a dog, I'd name him Spot."

"Or Bandit," Daniel said.

I stopped cutting the pie and looked at him. "Bandit?"

"We had a dog named Bandit when I was growing up."

"Ah," I said, moving the knife again. "That explains it."

"Explains what?"

"Nothing." I shook my head.

"The lady has secrets," Daniel whispered to Biscuit.

I laughed and Biscuit nuzzled his hand.

Sitting at the breakfast table with Daniel eating cold apple pie felt nice. Not natural, exactly, but nice.

He was funny and I appreciated his efforts to make me laugh after we read the sad letter.

It was heartbreaking to think that a young man named Benjamin had written letters to his sweetheart—lots of letters—and she had never read them.

"If she never read the letters?" I asked. "How do you think they got inside the hidden compartment in the desk?"

"I don't know," he said. "This pie is so good."

"I'll let Cook know."

"Is it the same cook? I think her name was... Opal?"

"Wow. You have a good memory. Yes. Opal."

"Is she here today? I'll compliment her myself."

"She has the day off. She'll be back tomorrow I think."

"Well. Next time I see her, I'll be sure and compliment her myself, too."

"That would be nice," I said. "She'd like that."

Although I said the words calmly, my blood was pounding in my ears.

It was such a little thing. Inconsequential really.

But Daniel saying he would see Cook again implied that he would be here again.

Just a small thing, really.

And yet it carried so much weight for me.

I sat back in my chair and watched him eat.

He was so handsome. Even just wearing jeans and a sweatshirt, his face gone unshaven for the day, he looked like he just stepped out of a magazine.

He looked every bit the handsome pilot he was.

The crush I'd had on him when I was nine years old hadn't dimmed. It had quite simply been simmering in the background.

Just the fire he had brought back to life so easily, just by being here, he'd brought my crush back to life again.

"So has the desk always been in your family?" he asked.

"As far as I know."

"Hmm." He shoved his empty plate aside and looked at me. "That should make it easier. Do you know if there's an old family Bible around somewhere?"

"Probably," I said. "Maybe in the attic."

"It would be interesting to know who they were," he said. "Benjamin and Abigail."

"Yes. I would agree. Do you want to go up there and look?"

"Thought you'd never ask," he said.

Biscuit barked three times.

"I think that means he wants to go outside," I said.

"I'll take him."

Tail wagging happily, Biscuit went to the back door with Daniel and waited while Daniel hooked up his leash.

I didn't bother telling him that Tori let him run free outside. It was definitely best not to lose Biscuit on our watch.

I watched them walk around for a few minutes, then put our pie plates in the dishwasher.

How was it that Daniel had just slid right back into my life?

I had to be careful. I had to guard my heart.

But for today, at least, today I could just live in the moment. Today I could enjoy spending time with the man who'd had my heart since I was nine years old.

Chapter Thirty

DANIEL

Sometimes I missed the simple things. Like taking a dog for a walk. I should have worn my jacket, but it wasn't too bad outside for a few minutes.

The dog took right to me, acting like we'd been old friends forever.

He was just a puppy really. A big overgrown puppy.

The letters Bella and I had found in the secret compartment in the desk were a mystery. A sad mystery.

We'd probably never know who Benjamin and Abigail were.

Benjamin obviously loved her very much even though they had been separated by war.

I wondered if they were ever reunited, but I doubted it.

Something had happened for the letter to still be sealed.

I could put myself in Benjamin's shoes. I hadn't gone to war and I hadn't written letters to Bella, but I could have. I had certainly thought about her.

And no one else had ever snagged my heart.

So, yes, I could definitely put myself in his shoes.

I was fortunate that I had run into Bella again.

It could have just as easily gone the other way. I could just as easily have never seen Bella again.

I didn't want to think about that version of my life.

Now that I had found her again, I didn't want to lose her.

I didn't know how to avoid it.

In truth I might not be able to avoid it.

But I would take it one day at the time. One moment at the time.

We would see what would be.

"Come on, Biscuit," I said. "Let's not keep the lady waiting."

Biscuit and I walked back toward the house. I walked. Biscuit trotted.

I'd grown up in Pittsburgh. In the city. And after that I'd moved to Houston.

I was a city boy through and through and yet there was something relaxing about being here with Bella. In the peaceful quiet.

I could see myself with her. Living here. Owning a dog.

Going back inside, I unhooked Biscuit's leash and he ran straight to Bella.

Barked once.

"Did you have a good time?" Bella asked him.

"I think he has a good time wherever he is."

"It's a good trait to have," she said. "Are you ready to venture up into the attic?"

"Are you sure it's safe?" I asked.

"Safe?" She leaned her head to the side.

"Attics in old houses like this are usually haunted, aren't they?" I asked.

"I think you read too much."

"I don't like to rule out any possibilities."

She looked at me sideways.

"Good to know," she said. "We can take Biscuit if it makes you feel safer."

"I don't mind if Biscuit goes," I said. "He's my buddy."

"Okay then," she said. "Here we go."

Chapter Thirty-One

ISABELLA

The door leading up to the attic was on the third floor.

I had never really cared much for attics.

They were dusty and cluttered and held a bunch of old things no one wanted anymore.

I liked my antique desk that my grandmother had given me and I had an old Tiffany lamp in my bedroom, but I didn't see the point in keeping things like discarded lampshades and boxes of old clothes that had been out of style for years.

I was something of a minimalist. I liked things clean and simple. Organized.

The door creaked as I opened it and the three of us started up the narrow wooden stairs. Biscuit took the lead.

"Not my favorite place," I said.

"I told you," he said.

"The house isn't known for being haunted," I said.

"Maybe the ghosts are just laying low. Waiting for someone unsuspecting to come along."

"You're silly."

He suddenly put both hands on my waist. I squealed and nearly lost my balance. He deftly caught me.

"See?" he said. "Scary."

"Are you trying to get us both killed?" I asked.

"Now who's being dramatic?"

We reached the top of the stairs and I switched on the overhead light. It blinked once, then turned on.

The attic was everything I expected.

Dark and musty. Filled with things that no one wanted.

"How did they get this furniture up here?" Daniel wondered.

"I honestly don't know."

There was what looked a sofa covered with a sheet. At first glance, it looked too wide to come up the narrow stairs.

In addition, there were some spider webs hanging from the ceiling. I found that particularly disturbing since spider webs typically meant there were spiders about.

"You okay?" Daniel asked.

"Spiders."

"Understood. I'll keep an eye out. Any idea where we should start?"

"Probably an old trunk if we can find one."

"Mind if I look around?"

"Please do," I said, rubbing my arms. The attic obviously wasn't heated. We should have worn jackets.

Sunlight streamed in through the dormer window on the west side, creating a sparkle of dust.

As Daniel wandered around looking for a trunk, I walked over to the window through the dust sparkles and looked outside.

It was a beautiful autumn day. The red maple leaves fluttered in the wind, one by one gliding their way to the ground. So beautiful. So peaceful.

It was better here with Daniel, I decided.

I wasn't afraid to be in the attic.

I realized with a start that I wasn't afraid of much of anything as long as Daniel was here.

Not even spiders.

Chapter Thirty-Two

DANIEL

The old attic was crowded with things that had probably been stuck up here decades ago and forgotten. Maybe even longer than decades for some things.

There was a couch covered with a dusty sheet that looked too big to come up the narrow stairs, but somehow someone had gotten it up here anyway.

It didn't smell as bad as I had expected. A little musty, but someone must have aired it out recently. Maybe opened one of the three dormer windows.

I found a trunk that looked promising, but it was locked. I decided it was the most likely place for old family papers and maybe even an old family Bible.

Looking around for Bella, I didn't see her at first.

I felt a little surge of panic, illogical that it might be, that something had happened to her.

But then I saw her standing in front of the westernmost window on the other side of sun sparkles.

She had her back to me, but turned around as I approached her.

With the dusty sunlight sparkling around her, she looked like an ethereal being.

I took a deep breath and walked through the dust sparkles to her.

As I put a hand on her elbow, she tilted her chin up to look into my eyes.

"Bella," I said, her name little more than a whisper.

Her green eyes sparkled in the afternoon sunlight. She was no siren now.

I was already under her spell.

"Did you find something?" she asked.

"Yes," I said. She was asking about the trunk, but I was talking about her.

I'd found her.

It had been her all along.

Deep in my heart I'd known it all along, but now I knew it without a doubt.

"A trunk?" she asked.

"I found a trunk," I said. "But it's locked."

"Locked?" She pressed her fingertips against her forehead. "Why would someone lock a trunk up here?"

"Why would someone hide letters in a secret compartment in a desk?"

"I don't know," she said with a little shrug.

Then she smiled at me.

She smiled and I felt the tug deep inside.

"Bella," I said, running a hand down her arm to take her hand in mine.

I lifted her hand. Kissed her palm.

She put her other hand on my shoulder.

I had found my reason for being here. With her.

I had never stopped loving her.

I never would.

Placing a hand gently on her chin, I slowly lowered my lips toward hers.

I'd kissed her quickly and boldly when I was nine.

Oddly enough, I wasn't feeling that now.

Our breath mingled.

Her eyes fluttered closed.

Then I pressed my lips lightly against hers.

Chapter Thirty-Three

Isabella

I watched Daniel walk toward me, Biscuit at his feet.

He walked straight through the sparkling sunlight, stopped in front of me, and took my hand.

He whispered my name, letting loose a bevy of butterflies in my stomach.

Standing in the sunlight with Daniel holding my hand, I looked into his sparkling blue eyes.

He looked at me with such an intensity that it nearly took my breath away.

When he kissed the palm of my hand I nearly came undone.

Daniel was the man of my fantasies.

Since I was nine years old.

Since then when I imagined myself with someone, I imagined myself with him.

He'd been the knight in shining armor of my dreams. The man I compared all other men to.

And he was here. Right here.

When he lowered his head to mine, my eyes drifted closed and his breath mingled with mine.

He smelled like blue spruce trees after a rain with just a very faint hint of jet fuel beneath it. Or maybe it was paint. Either way he'd recently showered.

I wanted him to kiss me more than I wanted to take the next breath.

I didn't think I could bear it if he didn't kiss me.

When his lips touched mine, I sank into the kiss. Leaning toward him, it was his strength that kept my knees from giving out beneath me.

We stood that way, his lips lightly pressed against mine as the seconds passed.

Maybe it was minutes.

Maybe it was forever.

Pulling back, he searched my eyes.

"Isabella," he said.

Hearing my name, my full name, on his lips snagged something loose inside me.

I wrapped my arms around him and pressed my lips against his again.

One of us, probably both of us, deepened the kiss.

I don't know how long we stood there, but when I opened my eyes, the sun had shifted, leaving us in shadows.

I heard a car door slam outside, then a second one.

One of my brothers was home.

"Will someone come looking for us?" Daniel asked.

"I don't think so." I moistened my lips with my tongue. "We give each other privacy."

"In that case, we need to go downstairs."

"Why?" My brain was foggy or maybe he just wasn't making any sense.

"I don't care to have one of your brothers kick my ass."

I laughed.

"I don't think that's going to happen."

"Nonetheless, I'm not willing to risk ruining your reputation."

He started toward the door, pulling me with him. Biscuit trotted along at our heels.

Apparently, Daniel was a gentleman.

And it was quite possible that he belonged in an earlier century.

Thinking about that reminded me of the letters we had started reading.

We still didn't know who Benjamin and Abigail were.

We might never know.

But right now it didn't matter.

Right now all that mattered was that Daniel was here.

He had kissed me and nothing would ever be the same again.

Chapter Thirty-Four

DANIEL

"There he is," Tori said, kneeling down. Biscuit bounded toward her with obvious joy and licked her face.

"How's it going?" James asked when he saw us coming along behind the dog.

"Good," I said. "That's a good dog you have there."

"Tori's dog as you can see."

"He's your dog, too," Tori insisted.

"Tori," Bella said. "Have you met Daniel?"

"No," Tori said, standing up, holding out a hand. "I don't think so. Nice to meet you."

"You too," Daniel said. "Congratulations on getting married."

James pulled Tori into a hug. Kissed her top of the head.

"So..." James said. "What are you two up to?"

"Can I tell him?" Daniel asked me.

"Sure," Bella said with a shrug.

"Bella and I found some old letters in a hidden compartment in her desk."

"Sounds intriguing," Tori said.

"They were written in the 1860s by someone named Benjamin to someone named Abigail."

"They were still sealed," Daniel said. "We don't think Abigail ever read them."

"We went into the attic to see if we could find out who Benjamin and Abigail are."

"Guess that's where our brother Benjamin got his name," James said.

Bella glanced at me.

"I didn't think about that."

"Actually," James said. "I think I can help you with that. There's an old family Bible in Father's study."

"The study," Bella said, looking at me. "I didn't think about that either."

"It's not as dramatic as the attic," Daniel said with a little smile that brought a flush to my cheeks along with memory of his lips against mine.

"I'm going to take Biscuit outside," Tori said.

"How quickly they forget," I said as Biscuit pranced along following Tori to the door.

"I wouldn't take it personally," Bella said. "I think you made a new friend anyway."

James looked at me and Bella.

"I'll go see what I can find," he said. "Be back in a few minutes."

After James walked off toward the study, I leaned over and whispered to Bella.

"I think he's onto us."

"You think?" she said with a little smile.

"Yes. But I think it's okay."

She nodded slowly.

"Why are you looking at me like that?" I asked.

"I've just never known anyone like you," she said.

When I looked at her questioningly, she clarified.

"I've never known anyone to care one way or another about someone's reputation."

"You've been hanging around with the wrong people."

"I think you're right."

"Don't worry," I said, putting an arm around her. "I've got you."

James was coming back down the hallway.

"I found something," he said.

Bella and I would have to continue this conversation later.

Right now we had a mystery to solve.

Chapter Thirty-Five

ISABELLA

Daniel and I sat next to each other on the sofa in front of the fireplace.

My brother, James, was appropriately baffled when we showed him the letters we'd found.

"If no one ever read them?" he asked, carefully flipping through them. "Why were they hidden away like that?"

"That's what we can't figure out."

"There are fifty-two of them," James said, setting the stack of letters back on the coffee table.

"He must have written her every month," I said, picking up the letters and looking at the dates, but the print was faded. "We'd have to open them to see the dates."

"Well," Daniel said. "Before we do that, let's see if they're in here." He slid the large Bible toward him and opened it up to the middle.

"You act you've done this before," I said.

"Maybe," James said. "Maybe I was curious about my ancestors."

I'd never really been curious about people in history. It never really occurred to me to be. It never occurred to me that I might have people in my past who had been in similar situations to me.

Benjamin had obviously loved Abigail very much. It was likely that Abigail loved him as well, but something had happened. Something other than the obvious—the war.

Something had happened that had prevented Abigail from opening her letters.

"Look," James said. "I found them."

"Tell us," Daniel said.

James read silently for a moment then looked up. Tori came and sat down next to him, Biscuit sitting at her feet.

"They were married," James said, taking his wife's hand.

"When?" I asked.

"March 5, 1861," he said.

"That was right before the war started," Daniel said.

"You know your history," I said, looking at Daniel with surprise.

"I know a little about a lot of things. I have a good memory for trivia."

James was scowling.

"There's a note here. Shortly after Benjamin left for the war, she left. She went home. To her family."

"He sent the letters here," I said. "But she wasn't here to get them."

"Or read them," Daniel said.

"No," James said, reading again. "Something happened."

We all sat quietly waiting for James to continue.

"She never came home. She never read the letters."

"And someone hid the letters for her," Daniel said.

"But why?" I asked, not realizing it was out loud.

"We'll never know," Tori said.

I looked at Daniel.

James took a breath and continued. "She died in childbirth."

A silence hung over the room.

A log burned in two, sending out a spray of sparks.

"We have to read the rest of the letters," I said. "We have to do it for her. And for him."

"I agree."

"She never came home," Tori said. Tori's eyes were moist.

James pulled her close. Kissed her on the cheek.

"What happened after that?" I asked. "To the baby?"

Daniel scanned the page.

"It doesn't say. But..." He looked up, his eyes touching each of us in turn.

"Benjamin was an only child. So somehow he ended up with the baby here.'"

"He remarried," Tori said.

"What?"

"Look," Tori said. "He married again in 1867. They must have raised the baby as their own."

"This makes me so sad," I said. "I'm not sure I can stand to read the letters."

"We don't have to do anything today," Daniel said.

"We were about to order pizza," James said. "You two want to join us?"

Chapter Thirty-Six

DANIEL

We had a companionable pizza dinner. The four of us. James and Tori. Me and Bella.

It felt right.

James and Tori, still newlyweds, were cute together. Happy. And obviously deeply in love.

After dinner, James and Tori went outside to sit on the swing together.

I much preferred Bella's idea of sitting in front of the fire in the parlor.

She sat on one end of the sofa and pulled her feet up under her.

I sat down next to her.

"What are you thinking about?" I asked.

"Nothing," she said. "Just thinking about how sad it was that

Benjamin wrote all these letters to his new wife and she never got to read them. I guess there was no way for him to know that she had died."

"I wonder if he knew she was pregnant."

"Kinda of hard to say. Things were different back then." She picked up a throw and wrapped it around her

"I hope he knew," I said. "But he found out when he got back, I guess."

"Not really the same," Bella said. "At least he found out."

I put another log in the fire and flames shot up, sending new warmth through the room.

"It's a good reminder," I said. "to live in the moment."

"It is, isn't it?"

"Are you cold?" I asked.

"A little."

I moved closer, putting my arm around her. She sighed and rested her head on my shoulder.

"There's something I've been meaning to ask you about."

"What's that?" She adjusted the throw to snuggle in deeper.

"Do you happen to remember that day? Back when we were nine?"

She tilted her head so she could look up at me.

She was thinking, but I couldn't tell what she was thinking.

"That day when you climbed up in the tree to take a picture of baby birds?"

"Yes," I said with a laugh. "That day."

"I remember."

"Is that all you remember about it?"

"It seems I remember a few other things, too."

"Like?"

"I remember you kissed me," she said. "Then you declared us married."

"Forever and ever."

"Yes," she said. "Forever and ever."

"My grandmother told me it didn't work that way."

"You told your grandmother?"

"I had to tell someone. I was bursting with the news."

"I didn't tell anybody."

"Well. Anyway. Grandma told me that there was more involved. She said if I still loved you, I could marry you for real when we were old enough."

"That didn't happen."

"No. It didn't."

Not yet anyway.

We were old enough now and I still loved Bella.

Grandma was right that it was a lot more complicated than a kiss and a promise.

Chapter Thirty-Seven

ISABELLA

I sat snuggled under a fleece blanket in front of the fireplace, my head resting on Daniel's shoulder.

Since he liked a big fire, the flames glowed brightly, giving off warmth.

My brother and his wife had gone to sit outside. It was too cold, but, I don't know, maybe they found a way to keep warm.

I had begun to think that Daniel had forgotten about that day beneath the maple trees.

The day he had kissed me and declared us married.

Even at the tender age of nine, I had known that there was more to it than that, but that didn't keep the moment from branding itself on my psyche.

It was a relief that he remembered.

He didn't say what he thought about it now.

He had been so sure about it then.

So bold for a nine-year-old.

That kiss back then was nothing like the kiss we'd shared in the attic. Kisses. We'd shared kisses in the attic.

"What should we do with the letters?" he said.

"I still think we should read them." I took a deep breath. "Just not right now."

"Okay. Later. Maybe one a day."

"There are fifty-two of them," I pointed out.

"I know."

I did some math in my head.

"We'd have to read one a day for nearly the whole two months you're going to be here."

"Is that so bad?" he asked.

I smiled and looked at him. Then looked back into the flickering flames.

"No," I said. "It's not too bad."

"It's a plan then," he said. "We'll read one letter every day."

"So... what if you're on a flight?"

"Then I guess you'll have to wait until I can get here."

"You'd come out here every day? Just to read a letter?"

"It's actually on my way home from the airport. But it wouldn't be just to read a letter."

My heart skittered as I dared to think that the real reason Daniel wanted to read a letter each day was to have an excuse to see me.

"Okay," I said. "I can wait."

He lightly touched my chin and bent down to kiss me again.

"This," he said, his breath brushing against my lips. "This is real. This is now."

I knew what he meant.

He meant the letters belonged to someone else. Someone who had lived their lives.

And we had our lives to live.

Our lives were now.

We would make our own memories.

And hopefully there wouldn't be anything to separate us for any length of time.

I didn't want to think about what would happen when he went back to Houston.

That was one of those things I preferred to put off until later to think about.

Right now all I wanted to think about was Daniel, the grown up version, and the way he kissed me.

Chapter Thirty-Eight

DANIEL

I had a flight down to Cincinnati the next day. Skye Travels was not considered the biggest private airline company in the country for nothing. They stayed busy. Several flights a day busy. It explained why Noah needed someone to cover while one of his pilots was out, even here in his satellite division in Pittsburgh.

Fortunately it was a day trip and I was back in Pittsburgh before dark.

I would no doubt eventually have an overnight flight, but I'd deal with that when it happened.

I took the little Cessna in for a smooth landing. Taxied over to parking and went through my post flight checklist.

To say that I was happy about the way things were going was most definitely an understatement.

Fate had brought Bella back into my life and since I had a healthy respect for fate, I knew there had to be a reason for that.

I certainly was not going to ignore it.

I was going to spend as much time as I could with her.

I'd wanted to marry her when I was nine. I could honestly say that things hadn't changed since then, at least not that particular thing. But the reality that I could actually marry her if I wanted to, for real, had changed.

As I was finishing up, a text came in from my grandma.

> **GRANDMA**
> Are you okay?

> Just landed.

> **GRANDMA**
> I love the green walls in the breakfast room.

> I agree. It turned out nicely.

> **GRANDMA**
> Do you want me to make something for dinner?

Well hell. When I'd been thinking about seeing Bella every day, I'd failed to take into account that my grandmother was expecting to see more of me while I was here.

I quickly checked the schedule for tomorrow. I only had one quick morning flight.

> Can we make it tomorrow?

GRANDMA
Of course.

Tomorrow, I decided, I would take Bella over to meet Grandma.

Is it okay if I bring a friend?

Thought bubbles.

A commercial jet passed overhead, coming in for a landing, its engines deafening.

GRANDMA
Bella?

How did you know?

GRANDMA
I know my grandson.

I stuffed my iPad into my leather case and prepared to leave the plane.

GRANDMA
Of course you can bring her.

Thanks, Grandma. Talk to you later. Call if you need anything. Okay?

Grandma would understand. She knew how I'd felt about Bella all those years ago.

I realized I hadn't asked her about her date. I'd ask her tomorrow. Maybe if things went well, she would see more of him.

It was selfish of me, but if Grandma started dating someone, then she wouldn't be thinking about me so much.

I still had a ton of work to do on her house, but I'd get it done.

I could drag Bella along if she wasn't working. I had to remember that she had things to do, too.

We'd make it work.

And we'd see what the future held for us.

Fortunately we lived in a day and age when we didn't have to rely on letters to communicate and stay in touch. Letters that we didn't even know were received.

And yet I'd still lost touch with her for years. That ability to lose touch with someone might be harder to do in modern times, but it hadn't been eradicated.

I locked up the airplane and headed to my car.

Chapter Thirty-Nine

ISABELLA

A new query had come in overnight, so I drove into Robinson Township to meet with a potential new client.

The new client was a writer of cozy mystery novels who'd had some success, enough success that she had decided to go full time.

It helped that her husband was a businessman who could afford to hire a nanny for their two children.

Her real name was Maribelle, writing under a pen name I didn't recognize.

She showed me her little study where she worked. Books piled up everywhere. Stacked on the floor. Piled up on a bookcase. A playpen in the corner.

I didn't see how anyone could work under such conditions, so I understood why she wanted a place of her own that would at the same time keep her close at hand.

She gushed about my idea of building the office cottages.

We talked for about two hours over coffee. I made notes about what she was looking for and formulated a general outline in my head. She showed me the backyard where she was thinking of building her office.

Unlike Melissa and Liam's space, Maribelle's backyard space was smaller but she didn't have the trees. They had all been cut and the lawn perfected. Her building would be more straightforward.

Back home at my desk, while I sketched out some general plans, it occurred to me that she needed her office to be semi-attached.

A roofed walkway, I decided, with two or three foot barriers on either side to keep the snowdrifts out. She'd need an easy way to walk back and forth to the house to check on her babies. Even during snow storms.

That led me to thinking she needed a fireplace in her office cottage.

I lost track of time as I worked.

About three fifteen, my mother came to my office door.

"Hey," she said.

"Hi." I blinked and looked up.

"You have a visitor."

"I do?" My first thought was that I must have a client. But then I remembered that my website didn't list my address. I wasn't set up to have clients come here.

Momma put a hand on her hip and looked at me with a little smile.

"It's Daniel Benton," she said. "It's been a really long time since we've seen him."

"I know," I said, not thinking fast enough on my feet to tell her that she was running a few days behind.

"He's waiting in the kitchen for you."

"Okay. Thanks Momma. I'll be right down."

Suddenly feeling nervous, I put away my supplies and headed to my bedroom to check my makeup and run a brush through my hair.

My hands were shaking a little as I went downstairs and found him in the kitchen talking to Cook.

He looked right at home, the two of them laughing. When Cook slid a slice of pie over to Daniel, I laughed to myself. It was a wonder he wasn't big as a house.

"I don't get homemade apple pie in Houston," he said as I walked into the room. Of course he didn't. His family was scattered all over the country.

"Hi," I said.

"Hi." His face brightening, he stood up and came right over to sweep me into a hug. He wrapped his arms around me and lifted my feet off the ground. Right there in front of Cook.

"How are you?" he said, setting me on my feet.

"Okay," I said, having a bit of trouble catching my breath.

Cook laughed as he disappeared into the room behind the kitchen.

"I didn't know what time to expect you," I said, tucking my hair back behind my ears. It wasn't a criticism. It was simply an observation. It was Daniel's way to just show up unannounced. I was getting used to it.

Under normal circumstances I preferred more structure, but with Daniel, I didn't mind.

I didn't mind one bit. Oddly enough, I was simply happy to see him.

He gave me a quick kiss on the lips.

"I missed you," he said.

"You just saw me last night," I said with a little laugh.

"I still missed you," he said.

Me too. I missed him, too.

But I wasn't bold enough to tell him.

Not yet anyway.

Chapter Forty

DANIEL

I was getting used to the routine of spending my evenings with Bella, curled up on the sofa in front of the fireplace.

Tonight, though, was different in that we had dinner with her parents. When I had invited myself over, I hadn't accounted for her parents being there.

I knew them, of course, and they knew me. I just hadn't known them since I was a kid and not only was I grown up, but now I was dating their daughter.

Whether they knew I was dating Bella remained to be seen. I think they began to get the idea when we went into the parlor together.

I got the fire going again while Bella waited on the sofa, looking for dates on the letters in an attempt to put them in order.

"How do you feel today?" I asked. "Do you feel up to reading another one of Benjamin's letters?"

"I think so," she said. "It's what we agreed to do. One a day."

By the time I joined her on the sofa she had broken the seal on the next letter.

"Are they in order?" I asked.

"I can't tell," she said. "We have to just assume so."

"I wish I knew who hid them."

"Maybe Benjamin did," I said. "He got married again, but maybe he didn't want to get rid of the letters."

"Maybe. It must have been heartbreaking for him."

"I can't even imagine. Getting home from the war and finding out he had a son, but his wife had died giving birth."

She carefully opened up the letter, put on a pair of reading glasses and started to read.

"Read it out loud," I said.

"Right," she said with a quick glance in my direction.

July 3, 1861

She looked up at me.

"A month after his last letter."

I nodded and she kept reading.

My dearest Abigail,

I'm sitting here beneath a full moon, writing this letter by candlelight.

There is cannon fire in the distance. The scouts tell us it's the southerners trying to frighten us away.

It isn't working, of course. The southerners are bold and brash and full of spunk, but we have them outnumbered.

I wish I was at home with you and not sitting here waiting for orders to go to battle.

I count the days... the hours... the minutes... until I see you again.

As I fall asleep at night, I think of your long silky hair and I dream of kissing your soft lips and feeling your breath, sweet as honey, mingle with mine.

Bella stopped and looked up at me.

"It feels like we're invading their privacy."

I laughed.

"I think it's sweet that he loved her so much."

"It's so private," she said.

"Is there more?"

"Actually no," she said.

Your love,
Benjamin

"It's a short letter," she said. "It was probably hard to write with a feather."

"I can only imagine. We have it easy, don't we? We can just send a text message."

She nodded slowly, looking over at me sideways.

"I can see you thinking," I said.

"You cannot." She carefully folded the letter and put it on the bottom of the stack.

"What are you thinking?" I asked, watching her deftly loop the ribbon back around the letters and tie it in a bow.

"You and I can't text," she said.

"Why not?"

"We don't have each other's numbers," she said, sending me a look.

I unlocked my phone, opened up my address book and handed it to her.

"You're right. Let's fix that now."

She typed in her number and handed her phone back to me.

I immediately dialed her number.

Her phone, resting on the couch next to her, vibrated.

"And now you have mine."

Biscuit came and stood at my feet. Barked once.

"Does that mean 'out'?" I asked.

"I think maybe it might," she said. "Looks like he picked you for his backup person."

"I'm good at being a backup," I said, getting up and going toward the back door, Biscuit happily trotting along beside me.

I grabbed his leash, hooked him and headed out back with him in tow.

I was quickly learning that Biscuit had a routine when he went outside. He obviously saw it as his job to make sure the yard was secure for the night. He walked all the way around the perimeter, then headed out beneath the maple trees in the middle of the yard to do his business.

As I stood in the backyard waiting for Biscuit, I looked back at the manor. Bella and her family didn't just live in a house. They lived in a manor.

The windows glowed cheerfully with light.

This was a home.

I thought about my apartment, looking out over the city of Houston. Looking out at all the strangers. People I would never meet. Didn't even want to meet, for the most part.

It occurred to me in that moment that my life in Houston was lonely.

Everything I wanted was right here.

Wherever Bella was was home.

Never one to hesitate when I made a decision, I took out my phone and sent Noah Worthington a text.

I was time I followed my heart.

Chapter Forty-One

ISABELLA

Waking early the next morning, I replayed last night in my head.

Since my parents were home, Daniel had been a perfect gentleman while we sat together in the parlor.

But the goodnight kiss he gave me outside the front door had left me weak in the knees.

I was in no hurry to get out of bed this morning. I had plenty of work I could do, but I was enjoying a feeling of wellbeing.

I jumped when my phone chimed with a text message. Maybe I was feeling a little guilty about not getting up at my usual time.

The message was from Daniel.

> DANIEL
>
> Making a flight to Philadelphia. See you tonight.

I smiled. Tonight he was taking me to meet his grandmother. We'd have dinner with her, then come back here and read our daily letter.

> Have a safe flight.

I was smitten.

Daniel was the one for me.

I had no more doubts about that, if I even ever had any.

Getting up and sliding into my slippers, I walked to the window and looked out over the backyard.

Biscuit was outside. Tori, the only one who let him out without a leash, must have let him out.

Daniel was good with Biscuit and Biscuit liked Daniel.

Daniel needed a dog.

And I needed Daniel.

I threw on some sweatpants and a sweatshirt then went up to my studio.

As I settled in to work, it occurred to me that I could work from anywhere.

I'd miss my family if I didn't live here, but I'd lived away from home when I was a college student and it hadn't been bad.

Having a pilot as a boyfriend... or more... would lessen the distance between here and Houston, I mused.

But I was getting ahead of myself.

Daniel hadn't said anything about me going back to Houston with him. Not a word.

But if he did...

If he did, I could do it.

In fact, it would be an adventure. Houston was a much bigger city than Pittsburgh and it would be fun to explore it.

With Daniel.

I needed to tell him. I needed to tell him that I didn't have to live here. that I could live anywhere.

It was too soon, I decided.

I would wait.

I would tell him later.

When the time was right.

In the meantime, having decided that I could live anyway was both a relief and a comfort.

I didn't have to let him go this time.

I could go with him.

My mind racing, I found it impossible to work.

I went back down to my bedroom and put on my running shoes. It was a good time to go for a jog.

Chapter Forty-Two

Isabella

Daniel's grandmother lived in a charming little house in an old part of Pittsburgh.

Daniel said it needed a lot of work, but I had to look closely to see it. He said he needed to paint the outside of the house. I saw a few spots peeling, but it wasn't noticeable to me except when he pointed it out.

The inside of her house was what one would expect from an older lady. Lots of photographs on the wall, including a couple I recognized of Daniel and his sister.

He'd already painted the breakfast nook in a sage green. I was impressed that he had such diverse talents and told him so.

"Daniel has always been the one who could do anything,"

Grandma Benton said. "If something needs to be fixed, he can figure out how to do it. He's not afraid to do anything."

"Grandma makes me sound like a superhero."

"To her you are," I said, nudging his shoulder.

"I hope you like vegetarian lasagna," Grandma Benton said. "They tell me it's my specialty."

She continued to happily chatter as she prepared dinner.

"How was your date?" Daniel asked her after we settled down to eat.

"Oh. I don't know if I would call it a date," she said, but her cheeks flushed a little.

"When are you going to see him again?" Daniel asked, taking a bite of the hot cheesy lasagna.

"Tomorrow night," she said. "We're going to a movie."

"It's a date," Daniel said, leaning over toward me.

"That sounds great. I can't remember the last time I went to a movie."

"Daniel," Grandma Benton said. "You should take Isabella to a movie."

She called me Isabella even though Daniel called me Bella.

"I will take her anywhere she wants to go," Daniel said causing my cheeks to flush similar to his grandmother's.

"There," Grandma Benton said. "All you have to do is to tell him."

I nodded.

I tried not to, but all I could think about was how Daniel would be leaving to go back to Houston in less than two months.

It wasn't long enough.

Then I reminded myself that I was willing to leave here.

"I'm trying to talk him into staying," Grandma Benton said. "Maybe you can have more luck with him than I have."

I glanced over at Daniel, but he was suddenly focused on his plate, not looking at either one of us.

"I'm sure Daniel is needed back in Houston," I said. "Two of my brothers work for Noah Worthington and they're always telling me how busy the Houston office is."

"I'm sure it is," Grandma Benton said. "But they need pilots here, too."

"Of course," I said. I didn't want to be disrespectful of Grandma Benton.

Oddly enough, Daniel wasn't saying anything. He was sitting out of the conversation not helping either one of us either way.

I could only imagine how much pressure he must get from her about moving back here. I didn't want to have any part of it.

After dinner, Daniel helped her clean up the kitchen, neither one of them would let me help, and we headed out.

"I'll see you soon," Grandma Benton said, giving me a quick hug.

"Okay," I said. "Take care of yourself."

I felt sad for Grandma Benton living all alone.

"I like your grandmother," I told Daniel as he navigated the traffic back in the direction of the bridge toward my house. "I hope she doesn't get too lonely."

"I don't think she does. She has a best friend she does everything with and now she has a boyfriend."

"Maybe," I said with a little smile. It seemed odd to think of an older lady like Grandma Benton having a boyfriend.

"I'm hoping it works out for her," Daniel said. "I worry about her being alone, too."

We drove through Pittsburgh, all lit up with its spectacular city skyline, crossed the bridge, and drove through the tunnel.

It was almost nine o'clock before we started down the long driveway leading to my house. The maple leaves fell like rain in the wind.

Autumn was my favorite time of year, but the one thing I didn't like about it was that soon the trees would be bare with winter.

Daniel pulled around the circle drive and put the car in park. Instead of hopping out to come around to open my door, he looked over at me.

"I want to talk to you about something my grandmother said."

"Okay," I said, forcing a tight smile while the tendrils of dread gripped at my gut. "Why don't we go inside where it's comfortable?"

He hesitated. Then. "Sure. I'll come around."

All I could think was that he was mad and felt like I'd ganged up on him with his grandmother about staying here.

I needed to explain to him that I didn't care about that. That I didn't want him to stay. I understood he didn't want to stay in Pittsburgh. That he had a life and a home in Houston.

That even if he and I had something here, I would be the one to move. The one to go with him.

By the time he opened the door, my hands were shaking. He wouldn't even look at me.

"Do you want to see if Cook has any pie?" I asked, desperate for something to lighten the mood.

"No," he said. "I had some earlier. He must have seen my face because he quickly added. "Maybe later."

As we settled onto the sofa in the parlor, I braced myself for him telling me how he had no intention of staying in Pittsburgh and maybe even how he didn't want to even talk about it.

I had to make him understand that I didn't want him to.

Chapter Forty-Three

DANIEL

Needing to do something with my hands and give myself a few minutes to think, I got up and stoked the fire. Added a log and got the fire blazing.

I hadn't wanted to tell Bella anything in front of my grandmother.

It hadn't seemed like the place to do it. It was a rather private thing between me and Bella. I didn't want her to feel pressured with my grandmother being part of the conversation.

Bella was acting a little nervous. I could only guess what that was about.

Not one to put things off, though, I was ready to have this conversation and move on.

When I finally got back to the sofa and sat down next to her, she was holding one of the letters, presumably the next one in the stack. I had all but forgotten about the letters.

"Can we hold off on the letter for a few minutes?" I asked.

"Of course." She set the letter aside and shifted toward me.

"I didn't want to say anything in front of my grandmother," I said.

"Of course," she said and I could see her thinking. "You have to leave to go back to Houston sooner than you thought."

"What? No. It's not that."

"Oh. Okay. I didn't want to be disrespectful of your grandmother in any way, but please don't think I was trying to pressure you into staying here." She said the words quickly, like she was trying to get them out all at once.

"I didn't think that at all," I said.

"Good." She sank back against the cushions in obvious relief.

"I've worked something out, but I didn't want to say anything to her until after I talked to you."

"Okay." She picked up one of the throw pillows and wrapped her arms around it.

"Noah has agreed to let me transfer to Pittsburgh. Permanently. But I didn't want to tell my grandmother until after I talked to you."

"But... why?"

"Why transfer or why talk to you first?"

She looked confused. In an adorable way.

"Both."

"Well..." I took her hand in mine. "I want to stay here because of you. But if you don't want me to stay, I didn't want to disappoint Grandma."

"Oh." She looked at me as though she couldn't quite grasp what I was trying to say. "I don't understand."

"I don't want to leave you," I said. "I want to stay here. In Pittsburgh. To be with you."

She smiled slowly, then she started laughing.

"What's so funny?"

"I 'um." She put a hand over her mouth to quell her laughter. "I had decided, but was waiting to tell you that if you wanted me to, I could move to Houston with you."

I grinned and pulled her into a hug.

"We're like the Gift of the Magi."

"The Gift of the—" She pulled back and looked into my eyes. "I guess we kind of are."

We had both been willing to give up our way of life to be with the other.

I kissed her then. Right on the lips.

"Will you be my girlfriend?" I asked.

"I don't think I ever stopped," she said.

"Forever and ever," I said.

Epilogue

Isabella
One Month Later

DANIEL and I walked hand in hand around the yard behind my house.

It was cloudy. White snow clouds from the looks of them. The way they were banking on the horizon.

A flock of black birds landed in the trees overhead, then after just a quick landing took off again, moving as one. Like a they were all connected with invisible tethers.

The air smelled like wood smoke coming from the fireplace. The wood smoke hung low, like the clouds, creating a layer of mist over the ground.

We had followed Biscuit, not wearing his leash, around the

perimeter, now he pranced along beside us as we walked beneath the maple trees.

Most of the red maple leaves had fallen, but there were still a few here and there on the limbs that hadn't fallen yet. It wouldn't be long. A week at most before the trees were completely bare.

Bare trees signified the beginning of the holidays. Thanksgiving was just around the corner.

Dashing ahead, Biscuit stopped at one of the large maple tree trunks and, looking up, starting barking.

"Whatcha got, Biscuit?" I asked.

"A squirrel," Daniel said as a little nut shell fell to the ground.

We stopped next to the tree and looked up. I didn't see a squirrel, but...

I glanced over at Daniel.

"Is this...?"

"Yes," he said with a definitive nod. "I think it is."

It was the very same tree Daniel had climbed up seventeen years ago to take a picture of baby birds.

The crook of the tree he had used to climb up into the tree was over our heads now. Too high to climb even if we wanted to.

"We should have carved our initials in it," I said.

"It's never too late," he said, pulling me into a hug. He wrapped his arms around me and turned in a circle, lifting me off the ground as he did so and one of my feet kicked back.

"Wow," I said, feeling breathless when he set me back on my feet.

"This is where it all started," he said.

"Yeah? I guess it is."

"You know what I think?" he asked. "I think it's a magical place."

"What makes you say—?"

A snowflake fell, landing on my eyelashes. Then others followed. Light, airy, innocent snowflakes.

The first snowfall of the season.

"There," Daniel said. "That proves it. It's magical."

"That is what they say about the first snowfall," I agreed.

Noticing the falling snow, Biscuit started running around, his head up, trying to catch a snowflake.

We laughed.

"He's never seen snow," I said.

"He likes it. It's been a long time since I saw snow."

He held me loosely wrapped in his arms, looking into my eyes.

"Do you think you're going to miss Houston?" I asked.

"Actually," he said, kissing the tip of my nose. "I'm looking forward to introducing you to the second best shopping in the country."

"Second best? Where is the best?"

"I don't know from personal experience, but according to Noah Worthington's daughters and granddaughters, New York is the best place to shop with Houston coming in a tight second."

"I've never been to New York," I said. "Or Houston."

"You are in for a treat," he said. "And if you don't find what you're looking for in Houston, I'll take you to New York."

"And what am I looking for?" I asked.

"Well," he said, swaying me ever so lightly in his arms. "It seems like you'll be wanting a wedding dress."

"Is that right? Why would I be wanting a wedding dress?"

"You might recall," he said. "We have some unfinished business from the last time I kissed you beneath this particular tree."

"I don't know," I said. "That was a really long time ago."

"And yet it feels like yesterday."

"It does, doesn't it?"

"I'm not so sure I did it right the first time," he said.

"Seemed right at the time."

"Well," he said. "Maybe we should make it official."

Biscuit sat in front of us. Barked once.

"Biscuit has spoken," he said, then he dropped to his knees, both my hands in his.

"Isabella," he said. "Will you marry me?"

My eyes filled with tears. I was going to cry. Right here. Right now. I couldn't stop the tears from falling.

"Yes," I said, giving up on fighting the tears. I let them stream down my face, but I was smiling.

He pulled me down onto his knee and leaning me back, kissed me on the lips.

This was no chaste kiss from a nine-year-old boy.

This was a kiss from a man. The man I was going to marry.

For real this time.

Even at nine, our vows were forever.

Keep Reading for a Preview of
The Princess and the Playboy...

KATHRYN KALEIGH

The Princess
and the
PLAYBOY

THE WORTHINGTONS

Preview

THE PRINCESS AND THE PLAYBOY

Prologue
Jade Sterling

STUDENTS AND THEIR PARENTS, along with a few zealous faculty members, walked up and down the college apartment hallways. Rolling carts piled high with belongings. Things collected over the years. Blankets. Books. Computers. Artifacts of an era.

Loud pop music spilled out of the open door of the apartment across from us adding to the bedlam.

The mood was boisterous and celebratory. It was graduation day. The day we had been working toward since the day we moved in, all bright eyed, eager, and terrified freshmen.

I'd known many of these students since Freshman day all the way through our college years.

My best friend, the one I had shared my space and even my life with for five years, sat on the edge of her bed putting forth a valiant effort at not crying.

Camila Alexander had been the perfect best friend for me. One of her best traits was that she did not ask too many questions.

Camila let me be myself. I had grown and learned a lot about myself. I wasn't sure that I would be the same person I was today without Camila.

I sat across from her and even though I felt a deep sadness, I kept my expression blank. Emotional regulation was something that had been drilled into my psyche since I could walk. My professors called me mature. It was the only way I knew how to be.

"Don't be sad, Camila," I said. "We'll stay in touch."

"But I won't see you." She swiped at her eyes. "You'll be in Portugal."

"Yes." Technically I would be at Sterling Palace Island. But Portugal was so very much easier to explain. "I know."

"You could stay here," she said, hopefully. "We could go into business together. Like we talked about."

"Maybe one day. Right now my family needs me." That part was true. It was time for me to start taking my place as steward of the island.

"Okay," Camila said, taking a deep breath and steeling herself. "You can always find me in Whiskey Springs."

"I know." I smiled. I had visited with Camila in the small town of Whiskey Springs. Even though I had to be home for Christmas every year, I had spent several pleasant summer holidays with her.

I liked Whiskey Springs. It was a tranquil town. Larger than Sterling Village, but it had a similar tranquil feel to it, yet instead of being on the coast, it was deep in the Rocky Mountains. At an eleva-

tion of over nine thousand feet, I had learned about bears, chip-
munks, and fireflies.

"Promise?" she asked.

"Pinky promise." I held up my pinky.

Camila smiled as she linked her pinky with mine.

Then she turned and scowled in the direction of the door.

"You have to go," she said. "Simon is here."

Preview

THE PRINCESS AND THE PLAYBOY

Chapter 1
Jade Sterling

Four Years Later

IT WAS A BEAUTIFUL DAY. What I thought of as an island day. The breeze coming in off the Atlanta bay brought the clean salty scent of the ocean with it. Seaweed. Salt. Wildflowers coming from the cliffs of the rugged coastline.

Egrets swooped low, making their presence known by their loud calls and the gentle swoosh of their wings.

I stepped out through the gate of the little cottage next to the ocean where I had been visiting one of the island's seafood vendors and hopped on the golf cart next to Simon, my driver. Simon, a forty-five year old man went everywhere with me.

I couldn't so much as step out the door without Simon being somewhere within view.

Oddly enough, I had more freedom inside the castle walls than outside. Or so it seemed. I'd heard rumors that there were cameras, but I had never found them.

Simon drove slowly over the lightly paved road that wound its way around the island cabins, sometimes veering next to the water, sometimes winding back around toward the center of the island.

"Your father wants to talk to you," Simon said.

"You're just now telling me this?" I asked.

Simon held up his cell phone.

"Right." I sucked in a breath. A summons from my father was never a good thing. "What does he want?"

"I'm sorry, Miss. I couldn't say."

I narrowed my eyes at this man who accompanied me on all my outside journeys. He knew what Father wanted. He just wasn't going to tell me.

As loyal as he was to me, he was twofold times more loyal to my father.

I always wondered what would happen if it came down to him making a choice between the two of us.

He stopped the golf cart in front of the door to the castle and I hopped off.

"Do you want me to come with you?" he asked.

"Why?" I asked. "Is it something really that bad?"

"Never mind," Simon said. "Go about your business."

I laughed and waved him off. Simon was faithful, but when it came to secrets, not so much.

Still, blood pounded in my ears as I went inside and headed

straight toward my father's study where I knew I would find him. His study was on the second floor with French doors thrown open, bringing in the outside. The outside concrete balcony was as big as the inside room, doubling the space where my father spent most of his time.

The house was big and drafty. Pleasantly cool in the summer though.

The house looked like what it was. The ancestral home of a king who had ruled alone for the past twenty years.

I had fond, if blurry memories of my mother. The time I spent with her had been happy times. We had gone on bicycle rides around the island and had picnics on the beach. Played in the ocean waves.

Then the sickness had taken her. It had all happened so fast.

My father had flown her to the best doctors, but it had done no good. She had never returned.

My father had done the best he could to raise a little girl on his own. He had employed the best people to bring me to adulthood.

And yet my life had never been the same.

"Come in," Father said, turning away from where he stood at the open balcony doors.

I went to stand next to him and together we watched a sailboat slowly make its way back toward the shoreline.

"Who's that?" I asked.

"Benson," he said.

"Ah. Of course. Benson loves the water."

"Like an egret."

I knew what he meant. Benson liked to hover over the water like an egret. He rarely caught anything. Not surprising since he so rarely actually fished.

"Simon said you wanted to see me."

"Yes," Father said. "Come. Sit with me."

I joined him on the balcony where a decanter of wine and two glasses were waiting. He had obviously been expecting me.

I took the glass of wine he offered, but instead of drinking it, I just held it.

My father had never been one for preamble.

"It is time for you to marry."

My father and I had never discussed the possibility and certainly not the mandate that I marry.

"Marry?" I never planned to marry.

My life, as I saw it, was laid out for me. I'd been to university. I had my degree. I knew what I had to do. What was expected of me.

"Yes."

"Who Father?" I made a sweep of my hand. "Who would you have me marry?" There was no one on the island appropriate for me to marry and he knew it. It went without saying.

"Do you remember my friend? Barnibus Cornwall?"

"Of course. He visited last summer."

"Well. Barnibus has a son in need of a wife."

It took everything I had to remain in control of my emotions in that moment.

Just because a man had a son in need of a wife did not mean that I had to be involved.

"They will arrive tomorrow and we will begin preparing for the wedding."

I was shaking my head.

"It's not optional Jade."

"Everything is optional." I said under my breath.

"I'm not getting any younger and neither are you. We need an heir."

I didn't care about heirs. He could give the island away if it meant I had to marry someone I had never even met. Someone whose father decided his son was in need of a wife.

"This is the twenty-first century," I reminded my father.

"And you are a princess. With responsibilities."

Preview

THE PRINCESS AND THE PLAYBOY

Chapter 2

Hudson St. Clair

I was what some people called a unicorn.

Like most things I encountered in life, I took it as a compliment.

The second youngest of six siblings, I was the only one of the six still unmarried.

No one had ever seemed concerned so much with our two sisters who always had managed to stay under the radar anyway.

It was the St. Clair boys who piqued the interest of the residents living in the small mountain town of Whiskey Springs.

Whiskey Springs began as a saloon in the mid-1800s. The town was named Whiskey Springs because there seemed to be a never ending supply of whiskey at that saloon.

No one really knew where the whiskey came from. Some

believed there was a still somewhere hidden in the hills and valleys. Others believed that the town was on a major trade route.

Others... well... some believed that it was magical. The little town's culture thrived on tales of romance and intrigue.

The little town that started with nothing more than a saloon had boomed with a General Store, a livery, and a blacksmith, then it slowed down and grew slowly, houses spilling into the sides of mountains, but never outgrowing the little valley tucked high in the Rocky Mountains outside of Denver.

Although Whiskey Springs came in at just over nine thousand feet in elevation, it was dwarfed by the tall rugged mountains surrounding it on three sides. That was probably part of what kept the town small. The steep, rugged cliffs were majestically beautiful, but since they didn't lend themselves to snow skiing, it didn't attract the usual skiers from Boulder. There were some nice hiking trails and lots of beautiful spots for photographers and artists, but the town was mostly known for its Christmas celebrations.

The St. Clair brothers all had similar features. Six feet tall. Lean and fit from working outside in the family's timber business. Strong jaws. Aristocratic noses tempered by quick charming smiles. Deep blue eyes.

No one older than a Gen X could tell us apart. It made for some interesting rumors.

None of them were true as far as anyone knew. People tended to take them with a grain of salt and often a good chuckle.

Being the last single St. Clair male, I was afforded a great many... opportunities.

It was common knowledge that the St. Clairs were old money.

Our great-great... great-great Grandfather Nathaniel St. Clair had built the manor that we all lived in.

He had built it while he waited for his mail order bride to arrive from France. Apparently he'd had an overabundance of time.

Some people called the house a castle and no one found it odd that the entire family lived there. That would be like faulting the royal family for living together in Buckingham Palace.

Not that we were royalty.

Tonight, however, we might have been mistaken for royalty.

Our parents had invited everyone in their social circle, everyone in their business circle, and a few others just because they could to come to St. Clair Manor for the soiree of the decade.

It wasn't a wedding. Our family had small private weddings. A person was just as married with a small private wedding as they were with a large lavish wedding designed only to impress others. My family had no interest in impressing others. Or so they said.

At the moment I saw reason to bring that into question.

Tonight we celebrated the first annual St. Clair Christmas Gala.

Guests, many of whom had flown in to the Whiskey Springs private airport from across the country, traveled to our home via chauffeured cars. The winding mountain road leading to the sprawling manor was decorated with festive lights casting a wide twinkling net across the blue spruce trees in the front and the row of towering pine trees behind them.

The fairy tale drive ended at the manor, the theme of clear twinkling lights continuing along the stone path to the door.

Once inside the house, guests were greeted by a live towering Christmas tree, a grand blue spruce, brought down from the north side of our property.

The lights on the tree twinkled in shades of pink and silver. The decorations, some of which were as old as the house itself blended with newer ones gifted by happy customers over the years and others collected with time.

Even the staircase banisters were wrapped with pink and silver garland. Everything blended together in an understated elegant way.

A string quartet sat on an outside balcony, sending a splash of classical music through the air along with waves of cold evening air. They mostly played the easily recognizable classics interspersed with newer renditions of festive music.

A team of chefs had been brought in to prepare a lavish feast that featured all sort of maple syrup desserts from our family's own maple syrup farm.

The desserts were displayed on our dining room table, where our Mother insisted we have dinner every night. Not tonight though. Tonight we mingled.

It was all very fitting. The St. Clairs were known for supplying not only the town, but also the area with firewood. Any family that had a real Christmas tree in their home got it from our Christmas tree farm. And now my next older brother Wyatt had started a maple tree syrup production.

Some called it a farm, but it was so much more. It was an elaborate system my brother had built himself to gather sap and turn it into syrup. He also had our sister-in-law giving tours and selling syrup to tourists and locals alike.

The St. Clairs were the biggest employer in Whiskey Springs and they hired local, gaining us even more loyalty from the townspeople.

"Why aren't you mingling?" My oldest brother Gregory asked, coming to stand next to me.

Like me, he wore a black tuxedo with a red ascot. Unlike me, it was rather obvious he rarely dressed in anything other than jeans and sweatshirts.

"Why aren't you?" I asked.

Gregory shrugged. "I have a wife for that." He lifted his champagne glass and after tilting it toward me, swirled it and took a sip.

I looked over at my brother and wondered how anyone, even the elderly Mrs. Miller could possibly confuse the two of us.

Gregory's nose was much longer and he looked the ten years older that he was.

"I'm not so sure that marriage agrees with you," I said. "It's turning you into a Neanderthal."

"I don't hear any complaints coming from Hallie."

"You got lucky when you convinced her to move here to be with you," I said.

"Indeed I did. Which lucky lady are you planning to dance with tonight?"

"I think I'll dance with Kelly McPherson."

He laughed out loud.

"I can't wait to see this," he said.

Kelly McPherson was a seventy-five year old spinster who had worked at the town's library her whole adult life and still worked there at least three days a week. Over the years she had donated a substantial amount of money to the town.

Her generosity had gone unnoticed and unrecognized until Mother had taken note of her at one of this year's planning committees for the Christmas festival.

"I've heard she's a good dancer," I said. I'd heard nothing of the sort. In fact, I was making this up on the fly to annoy my brother.

"You're such a tease," he said, then walked off.

I'd always heard that the truth hurts.

I did not consider myself a tease. It wasn't my fault that women found me interesting.

Still. Gregory's comment stung.

Shaking it off, I went in search of a maple syrup tart.

It was the specialty of one of the chefs working here tonight. And the tarts were extra special because they were made from maple syrup from our farm right here in Whiskey Springs.

Would it be so very wrong if I took the whole tray of them and hid them in my room for later?

It was a trick I'd learned when I was eight years old. If it worked then, surely it would work now. Being part of such a large family, a man learned at a tender age to do what he had to do.

Preview

THE PRINCESS AND THE PLAYBOY

Chapter 3
Jade

CAMILA and I climbed into the back seat of a new car with buttery leather seats and a chauffeur wearing a tuxedo with a top hat.

Apparently my college friend had achieved enough status in the little town to warrant a chauffeured ride out to the St. Clair's first annual Christmas Gala.

I had a hard time wrapping my head around having a first of anything. Where I was from every tradition was hundreds of years old.

Including the tradition that heirs must marry to make more heirs.

Somehow I had managed to deny that existence of that particular tradition until my father handed that mandate down to me.

It was dark already as we drove through the town of Whiskey

Springs. Everything was festively decorated. It was quite charming, if a little over the top.

I was used to that though. Americans did everything over the top. It was part of their allure.

Go big or go home.

"I am so glad you're here," Camila said, putting a hand over mine.

"Me too," I said with a little nod.

I felt more than a little overdressed as I rode in the back seat of the sedan to the St. Clair party. In the week I had been here, everyone I'd encountered wore jeans and sweatshirts.

It wasn't Camila's fault. I was the one who had brought my entire wardrobe. Well, technically I hadn't brought it. Technically Simon had brought it.

When Simon had found out I was leaving, he had made his choice.

He had chosen me.

"Does Simon have to go everywhere with us?" Camila leaned close and whispered.

"Yes," I said. "But don't mind him. Besides, if anyone tries to jump us, he'll stop them dead in their tracks."

Camila looked blankly at me a moment.

"The only thing that might try to jump us might be a bear."

"If that happens, you will be glad to have Simon along."

"Huh." Camila turned her attention to the soft twinkling lights draped across the trees along the St. Clair driveway. "It's beautiful. Like a fairy tale."

We would be there shortly.

I rearranged the silver silk of my long dress and adjusted the pale pink sash that ran over my shoulder, down to my waist where it was tied in a bow, the ends left to flutter at my side.

I'd made the mistake of letting Camila pick out my dress for the evening.

This was the kind of dress one wore to a ball on the island. One with the presence of dignitaries. Not a party in the little town of Whiskey Springs.

It wouldn't be so bad except that Camila's dress was completely different. Her dress was slim and stylish looking in sparkling navy.

"How well do you know the St. Clairs?" I asked.

Camila turned back to me, her smile bright.

"Well enough."

"You work with them, right? At your bank?"

Camila was the vice-president of the local family-run bank, an achievement rarely granted to people outside of the bank owner's family. It was quite a testament to her skill and ability to work with others that she had been promoted and so quickly.

Even though there was no one in the car with us other than the driver and Simon, she leaned close and lowered her voice.

"I'm one of their personal bankers. So. Yes. Close enough."

I nodded. "That's how you got the personal invitation."

"I'll introduce you," she said.

Pulling up to the front door, the driver stopped and put the car in park.

Both he and Simon hopped out and opened our respective doors.

"It feels like we're royalty, doesn't it?" Camila asked, looking over her shoulder at Simon following along behind us, as we walked together toward the door.

"A little bit," I said as one of the staff opened the door to the manor filled with festive Christmas music coming from a string quartet.

There was nothing unusual about it to me, but, of course, I didn't tell her.

I wasn't sure how Camila could know me for so long and not figure out or at least question why Simon had been there to pick me up from college after graduation and was here in Whiskey Springs with me now.

A live towering blue spruce Christmas tree, sparkling with pink and silver twinkling lights greeted us just inside the door.

"The lights match your dress," Camila said as we walked past the tree toward the ballroom.

I glanced down at my dress. They did indeed match.

In fact, my dress matched the theme of the house décor. The green garland wrapped around the staircase banner had silver and pink ribbons and bows.

I was feeling a little better about the dress I had worn. The men were all dressed in black tuxedos, but the women were dressed in all sorts of finery from slim, form-fitting dresses like Camila's to more traditional ball gowns like mine.

I inhaled deeply and kept my chin up.

I could do this. This was no different from one of the soirees my father held from time to time. The only difference, really, was that my role was more relaxed and I wasn't responsible for making sure everyone enjoyed themselves.

Tonight I could, actually, if I wanted to, enjoy myself without having to worry about the well-being of others. That would most definitely be a change of pace.

Glancing behind me, I saw that Simon, as he always did, had disappeared into the crowd.

Camila saw someone she knew and headed in their direction. With nothing else to do, I followed.

That's when I saw him.

The most handsome man in the room locked his gaze with mine and my breath hitched.

This was an unexpected situation. Perhaps this night was going to be more interesting than I had planned.

Keep Reading The Princess and the Playboy...

Kathryn Kaleigh writes sweet contemporary romance, time travel romance, and historical romance.

kathrynkaleigh.com

Printed in the USA
CPSIA information can be obtained
at www.ICGtesting.com
LVHW041343080924
790324LV00005B/247

9 798869 394019